# Demon's Web

## LAURA HAWKS

# DEDICATION

To all my fans and friends who have supported me and
continued to do so, I'm forever grateful.

To my mother… today and always you are  loved and
missed more than words can ever say.

TO THOSE LOST WHO NEED TO FIND
THEIR WAY……
TO THOSE SUFFERING AND FEELING
LIKE THEY ARE ALONE…. KNOW WE
ARE TOGETHER IN THE WORLDS WE
CREATE.

## Prologue

New Orleans. She stood there watching as people came and went, but it wasn't the humans she was noticing. It was the city itself. An old city, especially in the French Quarter, filled with an air of secrets and shrouded in mystery. A conundrum of old and new, of ancient and modern. Of tradition.

Sure, to some it was a place to party, get drunk and dance in the streets. To others, it was a place to buy pungent-smelling cigars, letting the bulbous smoke circle with adumbrations around their heads before it drifted skyward to dissipate among the low-lying clouds. Still to others, they were in and out of the various eateries sampling and indulging in the multitudes of Cajun and Creole cuisines scattered amongst the streets. Rich odors of spices, fish, meats and sugar would waft about her.

Yet, to her, it was an enigma. She had traveled the world over. All the states in North America, all of Canada and Mexico and most of Europe, Asia and Africa, but nowhere did it feel like New Orleans. The closest she could get without actually being here was the old walled-city of Quebec. Even then, she was very aware it was different. True, both cities were settled by the French and retained a strong sense of occupying colonization, but New Orleans was more than that. The city was as unique as they came, emitting an air of luxury, decadence and a grace of old which was lacking elsewhere. At least, as far as she was concerned.

As she stood there, the city came to life around her. Sounds of music and beer-bottle-top tap dancing abounded. People talking as they passed by. Hawkers calling out their services as they strolled past. Tourists would occasionally stop for the gold- or silver-painted mimes who stood perfectly still until someone dropped a green bill into their pail or box, coming to life only then to momentarily entertain. Many just kept walking, their agendas set for whatever purpose their business entailed, whether seeing the sights or working at one of the many places within the Quarter.

Through it all, she remained unmoving like the mimes. Still. Watching. Waiting. Soaking up the air about her. She knew she should move, but then, she wasn't sure exactly where she was supposed to go. For that matter, she wasn't sure where she had just been or why she was just standing here.

Despite knowing the city and the vibe it generated, or the fact that she had traveled the world in which she can compare it to, she was lost on everything else...including who she was.

# Chapter 1

Fifteen years ago:

Nether Realm:

Fourteen-year-old Logan stared out one of the very few windows in the only place he'd ever really known. As usual it was mostly dark, but then it was always mostly dark in the realm many called hell. Occasionally, as now, multicolored hues of light would dance through the atmosphere and the darkness would go to a twilight every now and again.

Logan knew sunlight, though. His father, the demon judge Azamel, would take him to other realms so he could learn more about the universe. Sometimes they were for educational projects, but most of the time they were to indoctrinate the young boy on various creatures and plants which prospered in the land of light.

However, his mother, Clarissa, never accompanied them on these excursions. In later years, Logan wondered why and would often ask his father about it. Azamel would inform his son Clarissa had some things she needed to get done and would go next time, or she needed the respite from her two men to just relax. Still other times, Logan would be informed his mother wanted her two favorite men to get to know each other better and have quality time together. Logan liked that response the best. He enjoyed spending time with his father, seeing the hustle and bustle of the other worlds. Whenever he was there, the sunlight and warmth seemed to radiate all around him and Logan enjoyed the sense of excitement, which was lacking in the world his father governed.

Through the window, the lights danced in the sky with a rainbow of colored ribbons swaying to a beat only they seemed to know. Logan was so busy gazing up at the spectacle he didn't realize, at first, there was a girl who appeared to be about ten years old staring up at him. She was so young, so innocent-appearing and alone, Logan instantly became alarmed for her well-being. It was neither safe nor smart to be outside of the walls which protected him in this realm.

Logan didn't know who or what she was, or even how she got there, but he acted on instinct running down the stairs. There were very few ways to gain entrance into the structure of Logan's home, less even than the amount of windows afforded to the massive stone building. The major entryway was the receiving chamber, opposite a pair of immense deformed-looking winged gargoyle statues flanking either side of the rough-hewn stone fireplace.

The statues appeared to be skeletons and Mel told his son once they were a species of fearsome demons who were part of his first execution and what he needed to defeat in order to tame this world. The petrified bones served as a warning to others that Azamel was not only demon judge but also, when needed, demon executioner. To get past Mel and his law was neither advisable nor intelligent. The doorway in the chamber served as a portal to the world of light, as well as to the other realms Logan had only heard about in passing or in his lessons.

The only other accessible threshold into the building was a door which led to a garden. The garden was Clarissa's greatest pride and joy. It was one of the few concessions Mel made for her to have, yet it only grew one thing: an immense, twisted thorny vine of black roses which bloomed all year long. Mel told his wife it was his way of making sure she got roses every day from him. As a result, Clarissa ventured into the garden daily under the protection of two guards who accompanied her each time, so she could cut some of the blossoms for the dining room and her bedroom. By the following day, they would have withered and died, so she would repeat the process all over again.

The few times Logan accompanied her, they had to remain within the garden walls and the guards were doubled. Being a curious, youthful boy, Logan wanted to venture outside of the garden. He wanted to explore the realm his father administered, but so often he was reminded it was not safe. His father had too many enemies and some skulked near the manor in hopes of catching Mel or his family off-guard. Many lurked within the realm unable to leave. At times, Logan was under the impression it served as a prison for these demons, but was later informed otherwise. The demons had free reign to be who they wanted to be and live in a place they were not condemned nor ridiculed. They could enjoy their lives fully while being in their natural state. However, like the human world of light, not all were good and decent. And when some tried to leave the realm, it was his father who had to restrain them. Those who succeeded in leaving were then hunted down only to be forcibly returned.

Some resented his father's control over the land. They wanted freedom to rein havoc in the Human Realm, or search for objects of old which held great power. As a result, there had been threats to Clarissa and his children: Trinity and Logan. None of which panned out, but Mel was in no way about to take any chances when it came to his new-found family. Azamel had been alone for eons, trusting no one, wanting no one. He focused solely on his duty, protecting the human race from the demons who wished them harm.

How many times had Logan heard the story of his parents meeting? How many times had Mel informed his son he was nothing until she came into his life? Mel had been betrayed by a woman he loved, by his very own mother, by his family, and even his best friend. He had found it better to just do without anyone close. The closest companion he had was his assistant, Shara. Even with her, he didn't confide much or expose himself in any way. He demanded something, she would see it accomplished; end of story. This was as complete as their relationship had ever gotten: a trusting, slightly affectionate accord between them. Shara knew Mel would keep her safe and she served him well.

Then, Mel had to hunt a demon who escaped into the land of the humans and who ventured to find a historic relic, which was what Clarissa had guarded. Logan was never told what it was or what it did. They both told him it was not relevant to the story.

Clarissa didn't trust Mel when she first met him, either, and Logan found it amusing whenever that part of the story came up. There were times the young werewolf would physically fight him in order to keep from getting close. However, their adventures to other dimensions and trying to keep apart from each other only served to develop a grudging respect, which flourished into a trust, which blossomed into a friendship and finally into a deep love. The kind of love one only reads about in the classic stories of old. Logan could see it, feel it every time his parents were together. It was like nothing else in the universe existed except the two of them and their children.

The point being, it was unsafe outside of the protective walls and there was a young girl out there by herself. Logan's youthful exuberance didn't give him pause as he burst through the door and to the back of the house, where his window overlooked. She was still there, turning to face him as if she was fully aware of where he would be emerging from.

Logan approached her, then was stunned to stillness when her eyes turned on him. They were so unique, so penetrating. A light brown with rich, orange and yellow specks, which seemed to glow with an inner light. They entranced him and he felt a feeling he had never felt before. His heart sped up, his hands became clammy, his mouth dry. He felt his cheeks redden up to his ears. He was flustered, his breath taken away as he gazed upon this unknown girl before him. He stood staring at her silently for several moments as he was so captivated by her. Long, black hair pulled back into a ponytail, her skin alabaster white. She still held the gawkiness of a young, pre-teen girl, but he knew she would mature into a gorgeous woman. Of everything though, it was her eyes that made his youthful body excited and protective all at the same time. It was only the sound of a distant howl that brought Logan back to his senses.

"Who are you?"

She reached for his arm, clasping it within her own grip. "Don't tell anyone you saw me," she pleaded, concern lacing her child's voice. "I know I'm not supposed to be here, but I wanted to see it. The black roses. I've never seen black roses and I have heard so much about them."

"They are my mother's," Logan stated simply, gazing around the open expanse behind the stone structure. He was becoming slightly anxious. "Come inside, where it's safe. We can talk then." He hoped if he could convince her to enter his home, neither of them would get caught and neither would get into dire straits, which might otherwise cause them to be punished.

"I can't. They will sense me. They will know I am here," she said simply. "I'll be in terrible trouble if they find out I'm here."

13

Logan shook his head. He was so confused. She was still gripping his arm and the contact of her touching him didn't help his current, disconcerted state.

"Please don't let them know I'm here. I just wanted to see the roses, but I don't want to get into trouble or get you into trouble for being here when I shouldn't be. I just had to see them. Black roses. I just had to come," she pleaded.

Logan scrubbed his face. It was a tell-tale sign of discomfort, which he learned from his father whenever Mel was about to give in to Clarissa even when he didn't want to, just to make her happy. Logan grabbed her hand and pulled her along towards the back of the house.

"At least tell me your name, so I know who I am taking these risks for."

"Jasmine."

"I'm Logan. How did you get here?"

Jasmine giggled, a gleeful sound. "There are many ways in and out of the realm, Logan. It's only your home that is so heavily protected."

"So you just decided this morning, 'Oh, I think I'll go and see the roses!'"

"Something like that." She again laughed, then gasped as she realized she was in the middle of the garden surrounded by massive, blooming black roses, the scent strong with the flowers.

Holding her arms apart, her hands down at her waist and opened, Jasmine twirled slowly around, taking it all in. A huge grin appeared on her face as she spun to observe the luscious garden.

"It's as amazing as I had imagined." She stopped and stared into his eyes. It was really the first time she had fully gazed upon him. His hair dark, his body lithe, his arms just beginning to develop into some semblance of muscles, but it was his eyes that captured her breath almost as much as the roses had. They were a vibrant turquoise, incredible and almost ethereal in the depth of color. "Thank you, Logan, for letting me see them. Smell them. You are so lucky to have this available to you every day."

"I never thought about it that way. I guess because I don't know anything different."

"Well, you are lucky to be able to visit this garden whenever you want. To smell these roses, unlike any other rose I have ever smelled. The black gives it a slightly different scent. Strong, intense, but sweet and dark. It's hard to explain."

"I'll have to investigate by smelling other roses the next time I go topside."

Jasmine tilted her head to the side as if listening to something only she could hear. She frowned as her focus came back to the young man in front of her. "I have to go before they notice I'm gone. Thank you, Logan, for allowing me to see this. For bringing me here."

Logan became antsy instantly. He didn't want Jasmine to go. "Wait!" he exclaimed, startling them both with the volume of his plea. "Wait," he said again, more calmly, and turned. His mother had shown him how to pick the blooms with a shear located nearby, so as not to ruin the vines, and he cut one for Jasmine, handing it to her. "You can have this. It won't last long, but it will remind you of coming here for a few minutes longer. And you are welcome to come back and see it. Whenever you want. I… I would like it if you came back."

"I would like that as well, Logan. Thank you again." She took the flower he offered her and then leaned in and pressed her lips to his.

She wasn't sure why she did. It was a spontaneous move on her part. She was sure the urge was a result of adrenaline for sneaking away, seeing the roses and meeting such an interesting boy who was sweet, unlike any of the douches she knew back home.

The touch of his lips against hers was startling. She felt her stomach lurch and tighten, dissimilar from anything she had ever felt before. What was this new sense she had of wanting more from this boy she just met? More time to get to know him? More opportunities to explore the garden and, of course, more time to kiss him and experience all the new feelings he evoked. She felt things she hadn't comprehended even existed until she leaned over and planted one on him. Uncertain of her own reaction, she turned and ran back to where she could return home.

Logan was stunned. His body responded in ways unfamiliar to him and he was surprised by the reaction. He had just started to lift his hands to wrap around her in order to deepen their kiss, but she had already broken free of it, turned and ran towards the back of the house and gods-only-knew where. He stood there, gazing at the nothingness that once was her, stunned she kissed him. His first kiss. Was it hers, too? When realization dawned on him she would not be returning, at least not tonight, he entered the house only to find Shara entering the back room and seeing him come from outside unescorted.

Shara stopped when she saw the young lad enter the house without any guards in attendance; a frown creased her brow. Dressed in a simple jeans and t-shirt, her dark hair pulled back tightly into a bun, she recently added glasses to her look. Shara said she didn't need them, other than she thought it gave her a more professional appearance and she liked that idea. It was her way to seem more mature now that there were children in the home for the past fourteen years.

Shara looked over her shoulder then rushed to Logan's side, pulling him into the room and shutting the door firmly, locking it.

"What in heaven's name were you doing out there? And alone? You are no longer a two-year-old. You know better than to leave the house without an escort. What were you doing outside anyways? What was so important you had to go out there?"

Logan tried to think quickly. He didn't want to get Jasmine in trouble, but he didn't want to lie, either. "I thought I saw someone out there. I didn't think. I just went to look." He hoped she wouldn't query him further. While it was a partial truth and considered only lying by omission, he prayed it would satisfy Shara. "I just didn't think. I'm very sorry. Please don't tell Mom or Dad."

Shara shook her head. "You know if they ask me, I have to tell them the truth. But, if they don't ask, I won't volunteer the information. You must be more careful, though."

Logan hugged the woman, whispering a thank you, before running back up to his room and to the window where he first saw Jasmine. He knew she would no longer be there, nor waiting for him. She would have headed back to wherever she was from, hopefully with more success than he had sneaking back into the house.

Shara watched him leave before looking around again warily. Once she was sure everything was taken care of and she wasn't being noticed, she continued down the corridor to the rooms below. It was where the demons were held when they had been caught trying to escape or committed some other crime. She traversed down here often in the days of old to find Azamel administering or overseeing the punishment of a prisoner personally.

It wasn't the prisons, however, where Shara was headed; it was the quarters just before them. Knocking lightly as she opened the door, she entered the room, shutting the door tightly behind her after double checking yet again that no one followed or saw her.

## Chapter 2

Five years ago:

Clarissa knocked on the door, before cracking it open to peer inside. Logan waved her in and she entered, shutting the door behind her.

"Good morning, my handsome son."

He laughed and kissed her cheek. "You only say that 'cause I am your only son."

"I say that because you have grown into a very handsome man who would turn any girl's head. And when they get to know how intelligent and sweet you are, they will lose their hearts forever." She reached over and cupped his cheek gently. "You have no idea how it has saddened me you have been trapped here and not out meeting the women of the world. It's not fair to you. You should be able to date and find the love of your life."

Logan scooped her up in a big hug, twirling her slightly. "You are the love of my life and always will be." He set her down and kissed her forehead. "However, I am sure you did not come into my room this morning for reaffirmation of a son's adoration for his mother."

Clarissa grinned up at him. Twenty-four and he was going to break every woman's heart. Logan had his father's rugged good looks. Dark hair, a strong chin and a well-developed form, but his most outstanding feature was a combination of both her and his father: his eyes. Where Clarissa's were a vibrant emerald green, Mel's were a stormy, icy blue, which sometimes seemed to glow with an inner light. Of course, that was when Mel wasn't so angry his demon threatened to come out. When that occurred, they would turn either yellow or red depending on the ferocity of his anger, something Logan had only seen once in his lifetime when he was four and very grateful for not having such a thing happen more often.

Logan had been very worried for several nights after seeing his father's demon rise up. Logan was very afraid a demon lived inside of him also, scared what it meant and when it might come out. Worse, he was afraid of what it might do if the demon inside were released, but both of his parents assured him he was demon free. The worst he could possibly be would be a wolf-shifter like his mother. After not sleeping for a couple of nights in fear of a demon emerging out of his young body, Azamel decided the young lad needed to know he was safe from having a creature hiding inside like his father.

Tucking the child into the safety of his arms, Mel explained things.

"Destruction, my demon's name, was given to me as a punishment for a crime I didn't commit," Mel told his young son as he tucked him into bed.

"Will you tell me what happened then?" Logan asked, his eyes wide with the anxious fear and curiosity of a youthful child.

Azamel hesitated. He wasn't quite sure this was something his son should know, but then again, he realized his son should understand the complexities of his own heritage. Mel sat down across from his son and began his story.

"I had just turned sixteen. Although my brother was older by two years, I was the more responsible, better liked sibling. Which in and of itself was amazing considering who our parents are: the god of the dead, Chipiapoos, and the goddess of evil, Beloitah.

"With parents like those, we weren't the most favored of kids or usually given the benefit of the doubt. We still needed to be trained in our given tasks for adulthood in preparation for the duties we would assume, the place we would take within the cosmos. The choice would be up to Chipiapoos' brother, Nanaboojoo, god of protecting humanity. He would be able to look into our souls and determine our place in the realm of the gods. This was usually done on our eighteenth birthday and my brother, your Uncle, Jes'Sakkid, was to undergo the ritual in a couple of days."

Mel continued telling the story of how he came to be the host body for the demon which was to reside within him. He had to find a way to let the story he had told only once before flow from his lips. He didn't wish to scare Logan, but he did want his young and impressionable offspring to understand that he would never punish his son as he was punished. Never subject him to accusations without getting the entire story and there would never be a time when he would allow his son to be punished by carrying a demon inside. Azamel knew first-hand how difficult it was to adapt to another thinking being inside, and more so how it felt to be betrayed by those he cared for and trusted. He would never expose his son to such atrocities or perfidies as he, himself, endured all those centuries ago.

Mel knew he had two years to go before it would be his turn to get his assignment from Nanaboojoo and he planned on making the most of his free time with Nokomis, who would later become the goddess of the crops. She was a beautiful maiden with long, black hair, which she always wore braided down to her hips, and flowers strewn about her head. She had large, doe-like eyes and skin as smooth and tan as the softest of calf skins. To Mel, she was pure perfection.

Azamel had planned a quiet picnic along a babbling brook to spend some private time with her. He had the blanket spread on the green field by the water under a shade tree. A rabbit was being roasted on an open fire spit as he waited for her to arrive. He leaned leisurely against the tree when he heard a sound in the brush. Quickly, he stood and held out a bouquet of wildflowers he had picked for her.

However, who came through the brush wasn't Nokomis but his parents, Nanaboojoo, Jes, Coyote and several other gods and goddesses. Mel dropped the flowers on the ground and wondered what was going on, totally surprised by this turn of events.

Nanaboojoo led the tribe, Mel's parents and his brother trailed behind him. The rest of the crowd was even further back. Mel moved to meet Nanaboojoo, standing strong and firm despite his youthfulness and uncertainty.

"Azamel, you have been accused of desecrating the sacred lands of your forefathers. What say you?"

Mel thought about how astonished he must have looked as he heard the accusation. It was absurd. "I say you're not correct. I have broken no laws, least of all being disrespectful to our ancestors."

Mel looked back at his parents, his brother. Surely they believed him? However, only accusing eyes from his own family greeted him in return and he felt worried for the first time in his life. He turned back to Nana, just as the elder materialized five dead deer, slaughtered and gutted. Nana then opened a satchel and unveiled a decorative ceremonial blade which Mel recognized immediately as having been given to him by his father on his tenth birthday. The metal was covered with dried blood. Deer's blood. Mel felt his stomach sink as he realized what the implications were.

"I didn't do this. I swear I didn't."

Coyote moved up to stand next to Jes and, with him, he had Nokomis by her hand. That alone tore Mel's heart to shreds. Mel knew Coyote also vied for Nokomis' attentions, but until that moment, Mel didn't think he had anything to be concerned about. Now, as he looked into her beautiful brown eyes, he saw only hatred. He didn't understand it. Why? What had he done to be accused thusly and not have anyone believe him?

"Is this not your dagger?" Nana asked him quietly.

"Yes. I did not kill those deer, though. I have not used the dagger for anything in the past week or so."

"Yet, it is covered in the blood of the sacred animals which roamed the holy lands. How do you explain this?"

Mel again looked around at the others. He searched for just one who would stand by him.

"When were they killed? Surely, the timeline will be my alibi."

Nana looked down at the carcasses and studied them for a moment silently before he raised his head to face Mel. "Twelve hours ago. Can you account for your whereabouts then?"

Mel almost breathed a sigh of relief. "I was with Nokomis then. We had spent the evening watching the stars on a blanket and discussing our future."

Mel was sure she would step forward now. He glanced over at her and bestowed a soft smile as he saw her move up to Nana. She would tell them the truth. She would vouch he did not do this dastardly deed. She leaned over and whispered into Nana's ear before she turned back to Mel and gave him a look of pure disgust before turning her back on him. His heart broke into a million pieces. She betrayed him? Did she not tell them he was with her?

Anger burned within him that she would be so cold. He loved her, did that not matter? He was innocent. Why did she lie? Why did she go off with Coyote? He was so astounded by the turn of events, he barely noticed Nana talking again as he watched Nokomis' retreating back.

*'Wait! What?'* His attention snapped back to Nana who was sentencing him. He was to carry a demon within. It would either consume him or Mel would find enough power to control it most times. For the times he lost the eternal battle with the demon, the beast would tear him to shreds over and over again, causing the most excruciating pain possible.

The others, his parents and brother included, circled around him and began chanting. A black mist from the earth swirled in answer to the call of the gods. Its wispy tentacles floated about, spinning as it rose up on Mel's body.

"No. I'm innocent. No. *NO! NO! NO!*" Mel screamed as the creature invaded his body, tearing and clawing its way into the sinews of muscles, down his spine and into Mel's very soul. The pain tore through him as he felt every shred of decency, love, peace and good be torn into such small pieces it was beyond recognition.

A part of him still remembered Coyote pulling Nokomis away and she willingly let him. How could she betray him like that? After everything they had shared, he thought she would stand by him, clear his name. What had she told Nana that sealed his fate for something he was innocent of? He died that day, or at least whatever humanity or soul he had perished.

"I will never see you suffer such a fate, my son. You will never carry such a despicable beast within you. You will never have to fight the battles I have or suffer as I have done. This is my promise to you, Logan. Your parents, unlike mine, will fight to protect you from everything that would hurt you. You are safe from ever having a demon within," Mel concluded before kissing his son on the forehead and shutting the door as he left.

Now, Clarissa stared into her son's eyes. She couldn't believe twenty-four years had gone by since she gave birth to him. Even as a babe, Clarissa was astounded by the color of his orbs. Logan's eyes mixed his parents' eye color for a very unique turquoise blue, which shimmered like the Caribbean Sea. His powers from his parentage began to show up after puberty, although he did not seem to have his mother's propensity to change into the form of a wolf. His father was a Native American god and Logan's magical abilities reflected that part of his heritage.

Unlike the demi-god status Logan now had, his mother was a werewolf, able to shift when needed or wanted. She rarely talked about her family, other than to state they all died by an attack from a neighboring pack of wolves. Whenever Clarissa did talk about her family, she always mentioned how grateful she had been to have had so many siblings. Her parents were loving and protective. As a result, she grew up with an open and loving heart. It was only after her family had been killed she became untrusting and suspicious of all around her.

By the time she met Azamel, who was hunting an escaped demon named Xon, she had a huge chip on her shoulder and no trust in anything or anyone, least of all any male who seemed to know so much about her and what she guarded. It took a lot of time together, Mel training her in her new powers and how to better protect the Gem of Avarice, of which she was the guardian. The time they spent together enabled her to trust him and he to trust her. He couldn't believe the kind, loving heart she seemed to have. And it took her time to believe Mel was actually there to help her and not take the gem for himself. Through many trials and tribulations, they ended up together with a love so deep it made up for the years of duplicity and deceptions they both endured throughout their lifetimes.

Clarissa reached for Logan's hands and held them as she pulled him to sit on the couch in his room. "You have not experienced much of the world, my son. Not the one I was raised in. Not the one of light and humans and a wonder which exists in that world. You have been trapped down here with us for pretty much all your life. I know there were exceptions to the rule. Your father taking you on trips to the Human Realm, showing you some things, but, it's not the same as living there and meeting people, good and bad. There is always good and bad in everything."

Clarissa paused and looked down at their hands linked together. Since she has been with Mel, her aging has stopped and she looked only slightly older than her son did at that moment. "I want you to experience the world, but your father is rather against it. He fears you will not be able to handle the deceptiveness of humans or the web of lies they create so effortlessly. However, I believe we have taught you well enough for you to not put your trust in everyone. Trust must be earned, not given away readily."

"Are you telling me to go out into the world? To explore on my own? Dad agreed to this?"

"He doesn't know. I'll break the news to him at a later date. But you need to live life and learn about the world and the others in it. You are old enough to handle anything which comes your way and I have taught you to control and use your powers, so if something out of the ordinary comes after you, I know you could handle it. Besides, if you find yourself in any real trouble, all you would have to do is call and your father would be there in an instant with reinforcements."

Logan thought about what this meant, what it would mean. He would be able to see Jasmine in the light of day. No more hiding. No more waiting for her to sneak away to visit him. He tried to steal away to meet her a couple of times, but it almost appeared as if they knew he was up to something as extra guards would arrive and man the portals. However, his mother was giving him permission to live on the surface and be with Jasmine, even though Clarissa was unaware of actually achieving such an objective for him. He tried to hide his excitement so she wouldn't become overtly suspicious.

Before he could respond in any way, there was another frantic knock on his door and, without waiting for permission, Shara entered. Her eyes were red with worry and concern. Without any preamble, she blurted out, "Trinity is gone. She was taken!"

Clarissa stood up, her face drained of all color. "Are you sure she is not just hiding? How do you know?"

"Zenthus. She wanted to go into the garden, so he and Jakome went with her, as per orders. They were waiting for her and jumped the guards. Jakome is dead and Zenthus is very badly hurt."

"Where is Zenthus?"

"In the infirmary."

"And Mel?"

Shara wrung her hands in consternation. "He had a meeting with Nana."

Clarissa frowned. A meeting with this particular god was rarely a good sign, but it was worse if Nana came to see Azamel instead of just calling for a conference.

## Chapter 3

Nanaboojoo was the eldest Native American god, the protector of humanity and forests. When he called a session, none dared to refuse. If he came to them, it was usually worse. Whatever he had to discuss would be of utmost importance, usually time sensitive, and very rarely would it be something good. Whatever he decreed, regardless of other's desires, was adhered to. Nana once told Azamel he could not be with Clarissa because Mel ruled the Nether Realm and Clarissa was a child of the human world and that was where she had to be. Mel was to train her and then send her back, away from him, forever. As much as Mel hated the idea, he obeyed Nana's wishes.

Once Clarissa was properly trained in using her powers and not letting her past get in the way of her fighting, he let her walk out of his realm and his life. It had been hard for both of them to adapt to a life without the other in it, but they managed. Azamel kept watch over Clarissa from afar, but didn't truly interfere. Clarissa continued to battle the demon hordes, which seemed to be thrown at her in search of the stone. It was only later discovered that Mel's brother was behind the innumerable attacks on Clarissa in hopes of finding a weakness in the young woman in order to achieve access to the Gem of Avarice, her charge to protect. With the power it would bestow upon him, Jes wanted to use the stone to overthrow Nana and take over the Elders Council.

It was only because of Clarissa's ultimate sacrifice in protecting the stone in the midst of an all-out war between the gods that Nana revoked his earlier decree and allowed the two of them to be together.

If Mel was with Nana, there was no way Clarissa or anyone would be able to get in touch with him until he returned. Normally, Clarissa would just let Shara deal with whatever the news was, but this was not just any tidbit of information; this was her daughter.

Logan blanched as he listened to the two women speak. He knew this was his onus: the possible result of an omission with his younger sister, Trinity, might have contributed to her being taken. His thoughts went back to a conversation they had just a couple of weeks ago.

He had just returned into the house and back up to his room, shutting the door after his visit with Jasmine. He took his shirt off just as Trinity entered his room, shutting the door behind her.

The youthful girl was sixteen, but still childish in many ways as far as Logan was concerned, even if he did adore her most of the time.

"Get out brat!"

Instead, Trinity continued farther into the room, acting cocky as she strutted about, tossing her dark hair behind her. As she did so, her soft-green eyes, paler than her mother's, shone brightly.

"You know Dad won't take me to Faefardom."

"That's 'cause you're too young in the first place and they don't like those of us related to Demonkin in their domain. Besides, why tell me this anyway?" Logan pulled on a fresh t-shirt as he watched his sibling saunter about, her nose arrogantly lifted in the air.

"I want you to take me."

Logan bust out laughing heartily. "And why would I want to do that, you little runt?"

"So I don't tell Mom and Papa about you doing kissy-face things in the garden with that girl."

Logan's eyes narrowed. "You scheming feral monkey-beast. I'll get you." He started to chase her but she ran to the other side of his bed, keeping it between them. Logan scuttled over it and grabbed the back of her shirt as she tried to get away. Trinity spun, the shirt twisting in his hands. She slapped at his fingers as she tried to get free, then stopped her struggling and glared up at him.

"Go ahead and hurt me. I'll tell Papa immediately. Then you'll be in big trouble."

Logan hesitated just before he released her. "What are you going to do? Keep blackmailing me for years?"

"Maybe."

"It's not going to work that way. I was going to talk to them about going to live on the surface for a while anyways. I am older now; it's time I get on my own. Once that happens, there won't be anything you can hold over my head to use."

"But until then, I have this. Just take me to Faedardom. A couple of hours. No one would know." Trinity knew from his hesitation she had won the argument and they would be going to the realm she was dying to visit. "Who is she? The girl in the garden? How do you know her?"

Logan sat on the edge of his bed, his face taking on a different, softer countenance as he thought about the woman his sister saw. "Her name is Jasmine. She came into the garden a few years ago to see Mom's roses. She comes every couple of weeks to see them and I get to see her. I don't know much about her, other than she lives in the world of the humans and she has to sneak away to visit."

In a sing song voice, Trinity teased him, dragging out the word love for a couple of octave changes. "You love her. Logan is in love. Logan is in love."

Logan, however, didn't buy into her teasing. Just the opposite, he stoically agreed. "I think I am. I mean, I don't know much about it and she is the only girl not related or part of this place I have met and gotten to know, but yeah. I think I am in love with her. She is sweet, kind, gentle. There is something about her that draws me to her. It's hard to explain, but one day you will understand."

Trinity watched him closely. She had never seen such a look of bliss on her brother's face. She could tell he was totally serious about this woman.

"And you don't know anything else about her? Why hasn't she told you more of who she is?"

"She is afraid of others finding out she comes here. She says if they knew, they would come for her here and she could die as a result. You can't tell anyone, Trin. If anyone found out, if Mom or Dad learned she came here, it would be bad. Very, very bad."

"I understand, Logan. I am not stupid. Besides, if I tell others about her, like Mom or Papa, you won't take me to Faedardom. I won't say anything. I promise."

"Fine then. I'll take you to the realm when it's safe to go. You know, when Dad is at a meeting and Mom is busy with the garden or some other chore."

"Fair enough," she said as she skipped out of his room, content she had gotten her way.

Now, Trinity has been taken from the same garden where he had his trysts with Jasmine. If someone else saw Jasmine there, someone other than Trinity, they could have assumed she would be on her way today. This would have been the right amount of time and, in actuality, Jasmine was supposed to arrive today for another clandestine visit. He knew from their previous meeting her plans today would be later than normal. She thought she might be delayed due to not being able to get away without notice, although she didn't specify why. He could only assume Trinity headed out to the garden at their normal rendezvous time to meet her, only to be taken.

Looking up, Logan realized the two women were still talking and his mother was becoming extremely anxious. He had to tell her the truth. He had to let her know about Jasmine, yet honestly he was terrified to do so. His little sister was gone, taken, and Jasmine could be, would be, next. As he gathered up the courage to, Clarissa and Shara sped out of his room and down the corridors to the infirmary. He rushed after the two women, his adrenaline high, his nerves taut. He was going to have a lot of explaining to do and he was not sure he was going to be able to do so to their satisfaction. Especially since, despite how much time over the past five years he had spent with Jasmine, he really didn't know anything personal about her: no last name, no family relations, no mutual associations. Hell, he wasn't even sure what kind of being she truly was.

Logan reached the doorway of the infirmary, something which was only as old as he was. Azamel never felt he needed one before Clarissa came. Demons either healed or died, it was the way of the world. However, Clarissa showed him a necessity, for herself and their children, should they require it. Plus, it was humane to have one for those who served him in the hunt and protection of the world. Mel relented to the woman he loved and had the most up-to-date infirmary established within the confines of his manor.

Most days the infirmary saw little to no action, but there were times, such as now, where it was a hustle-and-bustle of flourishing activity. Logan's mother and Shara entered only moments before he reached the threshold. Santanya was already there, holding Zenthus' fingers and leaning over him, brushing his hair back with her other hand, whispering softly to him.

Santanya looked up when the door opened for Shara and Clarissa, but instead of running and hiding as she normally would have done, she stood up and faced the small group, still holding Zenthus' appendages.

Clarissa peered over at Shara who suddenly found her shoes to be fascinating. So, the woman knew about Santanya and Zen. Clarissa wondered if Mel were aware of this odd relationship between them as well.

Santanya was brought to the manor as a prisoner, a tool to make Dzhihibai Manido talk. Santanya was Mani's mother, whom Mel realized was the leverage he needed to get Mani to confess who he had been hired by in order to eliminate the guardian of the Gem of Avarice. The guardian was, of course, Clarissa. With the full promise Santanya would be protected from harm, Mani confessed he was hired by Jes'Sakkid, who was Azamel's older brother.

The stone Clarissa had been assigned to protect was eons old. Her maternal family had been given the responsibility to keep it out of the hands of all creatures, be they gods, demons or others. It was too powerful to even exist; the temptation was too great for the potent influx of energy it would provide to those who wielded the gem. Clarissa's entire family had been murdered in order to achieve control of the stone she didn't even know existed until they were gone. She inherited the duties, which came with protecting the world from its influence.

It was why Clarissa and Azamel had met. Mel was hunting a demon named Xon, who had escaped from the Nether Realm. Xon was focused on hunting for the stone, which Mel could also sense once he reached topside searching for the demon himself. Mel agreed to help Clarissa in keeping the stone safe and away from Xon.

It wasn't until after Xon's demise, and still the battle for dominance of the stone continued, that Azamel realized there was someone else searching for the gem and therefore the guardian, putting Clarissa in harm's way. He had been forced to let her go back into the world, constantly fighting multitudes of demons set upon her. He had been unable to help by the order of the Elders Council, but that didn't mean he couldn't investigate on his own. He learned Mani was the demon who had sent Clarissa, and by extension, himself, to another realm where they barely survived, much less escaped. But, no matter the torture and punishment, Mel could not get him to talk. At least, until he realized Mani's weakness: the care for his mother, Santanya.

He had the woman brought to his realm and his manor, then to the dungeons so her son could see the woman for himself. Zenthus had held her when he brought her in to face Mani

Entering the small room, Mel appraised Mani still hanging from twin pillars. Mani's body was covered with scabs, dried blood and parts of his body had the skin torn completely away. Mel moved over to him and bent down slightly to make their eyes a bit more level.

"Any chance you will reveal the information I seek?"

Mani just shook his head no, keeping his eyes lowered. He knew he was in the wrong but he had to protect the deal he made even if it meant suffering for his knowledge. Mani heard the door open again but didn't pay much attention to it at first, until he heard a soft gasp from a voice he had not expected. He jerked his head up with the thought he must have heard incorrectly, only to be floored as she appeared before him, held by the most massive creature he had ever laid eyes on. His gaze fell upon the beautiful woman. Silky white hair with milky-white skin and colorless eyes. A true albino, he couldn't believe she was here in this hideous place, looking upon him with deep concern and sadness in her eyes. He turned his heated gaze upon Mel and scowled, his voice raspy from his earlier screams of agony. "How could you? Leave her out of this!"

Mel stepped over to the woman, his gaze appreciating her beauty. She was nothing like his Clarissa, but then no one was. Then he remembered, angrily, Clarissa wasn't his to claim.

"You brought her into this by refusing to give me the information I require."

Mel grabbed the woman's face and jerked it towards him. "She is why you're not talking, I would wager." He released her and sauntered back to Mani.

"I really don't wish to hurt her in any way but you may leave me no choice if you don't answer my question. I'll give you one more chance to respond. If you choose to continue your silence, then, well, you can watch as we employ the same techniques to her as we have been utilizing on you. The choice, ultimately, is yours."

Mani glowered at Azamel. *'How the fuck did he figure it out?'* He turned his gaze to his mother, Santanya, and his visage softened. She was so beautiful and she didn't deserve this. It was because of her he made the deal with Jes to begin with, the arrangement which he was now wholly regretting and suffering in silence for. He would endure any amount of pain to make sure she was safe and unharmed. However, what choice did he have now? He either gave up Jes and put his mother's life in danger later, or he remained silent and put her in danger now. It was a complete fubar situation. "You don't understand. If I tell you, she won't be safe."

Santanya squirmed out of Zenthus' grasp and ran over to Mani. She bent down and cupped his face in her hand before she released him as she turned back to Mel.

"Please. Let him go. Do whatever you want to me but please don't hurt him any longer." Her voice was soft and pleading, desperate to have him safeguarded as most mothers would protect their children.

"That's entirely up to him, Ma'am."

Mel looked back at Mani's mother. A delicate woman to be sure and he understood the need to protect her. That was, for the most part, what sons did. Well, except for him. He tried to murder his mother, but then she betrayed him and tried to kill him first. He gave himself a mental shake of his head. His mother was the queen of evil, literally, and not all maternal figures were that cold and cruel. Obviously, Mani's mother wasn't considering what he was willing to suffer for her, do for her. Mel raked his eyes over Santanya once more and wondered what it would have been like to have a mother who would do anything for him and who loved him. A mother who would give her very life to protect him instead of trying to eradicate him permanently.

Grasping her wrist, Mel yanked her away from Mani and tossed her back to Zenthus with a warning glance to the hunter to keep her still. Zenthus wrapped his beefy arm around her waist, keeping her immobile, her arms pinned at her side. Swiveling back to Mani, Azamel lowered his voice as he kept it neutral and nonchalant. "Tell me who sent you to put the Guardian into another hell realm. Tell me who you're protecting. I will make sure that neither he nor anyone else will touch your mother. She will be safe. You have my word of honor."

The entire pantheon and demon realm were aware of how Azamel's word meant everything. He, in all the millennia of time, had never rescinded his word when he gave it. Mani scrutinized Mel then glanced over to his mother before he hung loosely in supplication.

"On your word she will be protected from all harm, I'll submit to your inquisition with the responses you require."

"I already gave you my word. I am not one to repeat myself uselessly. Last chance. Who are you working for?"

Mani hesitated a few moments longer, weighing all his options, even though he was readily aware he had none. He sighed in resignation and uttered one word, "Jes'Sakkid."

Azamel gasped, before he quickly recovered and let the stoic mask fall across his features. *'Why am I surprised? Have I not been betrayed by all of them at one point or other? This is no different!'* Jes would want the stone for himself in order to overthrow Nanaboojoo and lead the Council of Gods. Jes was the god of Malignant Man, but aspired to be so much more. The Gem of Avarice would allow him to achieve all that plus anything else he so desired, once it was in his possession.

Turning on his heel, he called back to Zenthus, "See that Mani is imprisoned for thirty more days with the appropriate lashes given for his treachery. Then attend to Santanya by securing her a safe place within our realm where she will be untouched by those who might otherwise wish her harm."

Zenthus had moved Santanya to quarters near his so he could continue to watch over her. Nothing and nowhere was safer than this manor.

Zen also resided there as the head bailiff. He was the son of Boralium, once the best friend of Azamel's, but never knew the actual cause of death of either his parents. Mel made sure no one knew or would ever know as he took Zen under his wing to raise him. In time, the man earned his ranks to the head bailiff position.

He made many look small and puny against his massive size and demeanor. At six foot nine inches, his biceps were the size of cannons, his thighs as thick as oak trees. He had a low rumbling voice which boomed when he talked.

When Mel first took over his profession to hunt, judge, punish and even execute rogue demons who wanted to disrupt the human existence, Nana granted him assistance to successfully accomplish his job. The work was extensive, for many demons wished to roam the Human Realm, feasting on mankind as a snack. Mel was allowed to choose whomever he wanted to train as his crew. Of course, he chose one man whom he trusted more than most, a close friend and confidant he could discuss his problems with and who found women to be as untrustworthy as Mel did.

Zenthus' father, Boralium, stood by Mel through his transition of incorporating the demon into his body and finding a way to manage it. Boralium took him in when Mel's mother tried to kill him.

Mel would never forget Boralium's duplicity. He had just sat down with Boral late one evening over some roasted rabbit. To thank his friend for shelter, Mel willingly assisted with chores, including providing nourishment. Since the demon had been placed within Mel, his sustenance requirements had changed considerably. Although he could still eat and digest normal foods, Mel had different and special dietary requirements to actually survive as a result of the demon symbiont which resided within him.

Boralium was eerily quiet that particular evening. Mel wondered why, when his friend was usually talking his ear off, but didn't give it much thought beyond a passing rumination. Boral knew Mel was always available to listen should he decide to discuss whatever was on his mind.

As Mel sat back against the small boulder watching the fire burn, he remained quiet, enjoying the peacefulness which surrounded them.

Boralium stood and moved to the bushes. Mel relaxed and even shut his eyes for a few moments. The demon within had been particularly troublesome in remaining inside the past couple of days and Mel found the constant struggle exhausting.

As he reposed, he suddenly felt a sharp pain in his chest. Surprised, Azamel gazed down to see an arrow shaft protruding from his shirt, rapidly becoming stained with blood. It took Mel a moment to comprehend what occurred when two more arrows pierced his chest.

The demon inside roared as loudly as his host did. Mel's eyes immediately changed to an iridescent red as he gazed towards the location from where the shots were being fired. Pulling the shafts out, the tips still embedded inside his body, Mel scrambled behind the boulder, using the stone as a shelter. His powers forced the arrowheads out, his wounds slowly closing.

Mel realized there was some sort of poison on them, preventing his godly healing abilities to work effectively or quickly. Mel struggled to maintain control and not let the demon out but he knew the inner conflict he fought was a lost battle without his full powers.

Destruction had a reason to appear. He was being attacked and the natural response was to prevent any further damage to his host's body. Mel's voice was low and demonic as he called out to Boralium, "Boral! Help me!"

At first there was no answer as another arrow whizzed by then stillness enveloped the clearing before Azamel got a response, "I will help you, Azamel. I'll help you die."

Mel shook his head as he remembered how shocked he was to learn he couldn't rely on his friend, for it was Boralium who fired the arrows. The last vestige of hope died with him then. Furious at the betrayal, he let Destruction free from his interior cage.

Once the demon received permission, he tore through Mel's body, ripping sinew, muscles and bone to be liberated. Mel didn't fight against Destruction, so the demon didn't mutilate his host's body when he emerged.

With quickened strides, Destruction burst through the trees and was in front of Boralium before Boral was even aware of his approach. Destruction's massive claw wrapped around the man's throat and pulled him up off his feet to gaze eye to eye with the much smaller man.

"Why?" Destruction growled. "We were friends. You have done so much for us. Why?"

Boralium's feet swung as he tried to kick the massive beast. His hands clawed at the arm which held him chokingly aloft. "Because you killed the woman I loved and cherished. The mother to my son."

"You lie! You're not even married."

"I had a mistress in the other village. The village you raided two nights ago. You killed her and several others of her clan."

"Why did I not know about her?"

"Why should it have mattered? You're no longer a man. You're a monster, an abomination who should be eradicated."

Before Azamel could attempt to halt any further damage from Destruction, the beast savagely thrust his free claw into Boralium's chest, through his rib cage, as he ripped the spinal column from his friend out the front of his body.

"I don't get eradicated. I eliminate!" Destruction exclaimed.

Despite his torn up body and loss of blood, as well as his general weakened state from the poisoned arrows, Mel struggled to catch what was left of his friend before he collapsed.

When Azamel came to, Destruction had returned to his cage and he was healed enough to investigate Boralium's claims only to discover the truth of them. Zenthus was the son who was now an orphan by Destruction's hand.

Azamel took the child and raised him, never letting Zenthus know he was the cause of his parents' deaths.

## Chapter 4

Clarissa would have to talk to Mel about Santanya and Zen later, but for now, there was a larger issue at stake: that of her daughter missing, Jakome dead and Zenthus injured. At least the latter was alive to describe what happened and how she was going to get Trinity back. She strode over to the bedside, unconcerned at the moment of Santanya holding Zen's hand.

Shara held back slightly, moving close to Logan to whisper to him. "Don't tell them about the girl, Logan. There is no reason for either of you to cause any unnecessary agitation or distress over something which might not even be related. Your father has a multitude of enemies, any of which might have taken Trinity as leverage against him and not by mistake for your female."

It surprised Logan that Shara knew what he had planned on doing. However, he shouldn't have been all that astonished Shara was aware of Jasmine as well as everything else which went on in and around the house and its inhabitants. He leaned over and whispered back to Mel's assistant.

"Isn't it better if they know everything? What if it isn't Trinity they wanted but took her falsely? What if it's Jasmine they want and will use Trinity as leverage? Mom and Dad won't know what they are referring to in a negotiation if they don't know about Jasmine at all."

"And what exactly are you going to tell them, Logan? You don't know all that much about her, do you? All these years you have seen her a couple of times a week in the garden and most of that has been anything but talking. Do you know her last name? Where she lives? Who she is related to? Why someone is after her? What her powers are which permits her to travel to this realm so easily? Do you actually know anything about her of use?"

Logan frowned. Truth was, he didn't. She never wanted to talk about herself, never wanted him to know anything personal about her. Just in case, she always stated, and he never wanted to push her. Something about her called to him whenever she appeared. Something inside missed her terribly, but he didn't really have any information about her background. Shara was correct. What could he verbalize which wouldn't get them both in trouble or offer any respite from worry?

"I won't say anything, unless I feel it's important for them to know. Thanks, Shara."

Logan quietly followed Shara into the infirmary just in time to hear Zen's story of what happened in the garden.

"She insisted on going into the garden. Said she was going to be a surprise, but wouldn't elaborate. I insisted she wait for backup in guards, which she did. When Jakome arrived, we took her into the garden, both of us taking up the standard positions. At first it was quiet. Then there was a rumble to the outside entrance. Jak headed to see what was going on and I moved closer to Trinity. I tried to urge her to get back into the house, but she refused. She said it might be what she was waiting for and we were not going to stop her from it. The rest is a blur. There were a couple of them, but one seemed to stand out from the others."

"A couple of what? What were they?" Clarissa interrupted his description, almost frantic to get the knowledge out of him. "Who took my daughter?"

Just then, the door opened again and Mel strode in. If he could have looked any fiercer, Clarissa would not have been aware of it. She had not seen him that furious and upset in over a decade and she had forgotten how determined he could appear. His mouth was set in a stern, brook-no-nonsense line. He seemed to feel the need for his wife, as his arm went about her waist when he neared the bedside. It did not escape his notice that Santanya was still holding Zen's hand, a deeply concerned look on her face. She was the least of his concerns at the moment though. Mel waited for Zen to answer Clarissa's question.

"Rougarous. There were at least five of them. Three came in by Jak and he tried to hold them off, but…" Zen shook his head. "They were more vicious than I have ever seen. It all happened so fast. Jak was dead, Trinity was gone and I have failed you. I will accept whatever punishment you deem."

"Rougarou? Are you sure?" Mel asked astonished. He had no qualms with that species he was aware of. Why would they attack and take his daughter with no obvious provocation?

"I've never heard of it. What is a Rougarou?" Clarissa asked looking around at those there.

"They are creatures who live in the Maurepas Realm. A swamp world. They are half swamp creature with the head of a wolf. They occasionally have their world intersect with the swamps in Louisiana, which allows them to sometimes cross into the land of humans. However, they usually stay to themselves and in the areas of swamps until they can get back. I don't understand why they would have attacked here and taken Trinity." Mel patiently explained, though his mind was already planning on a visit to the Maurepas Realm to extract his daughter and behead those who were responsible for abducting her.

Clarissa took another look at Santanya. "Take care of Zen." She turned towards Mel. "Let me gear up and I will be ready to go."

"What makes you think you are going?" Azamel asked, disquieted by Clarissa.

"What makes you think I wouldn't?" she quipped back.

Mel shook his head. "You're right. I almost forgot how stubborn you are." He looked over his shoulder at Logan. "I suppose you will want to come as well?"

Logan gave a quick look at Shara to make sure she still felt he shouldn't say anything about Jasmine. In return, she gave an imperceptible nod. He still didn't feel right keeping this news from his parents

Logan nodded. "She's my sister and I will do whatever it takes to get her back."

"Alright. Reception room in fifteen minutes. Get whatever you are going to need." Without another word, Mel left the infirmary to prepare himself for battle with a species he previously never had issues with.

Coyote grumbled as he walked through the swampland grasses. He absolutely detested coming to this place and, if he had any other alternative, he'd never be here at all nor would he work with such disgusting creatures as the Rougarou. However, the lucrative opportunity far outweighed the abhorrent action of materializing at this realm.

He didn't pause or knock, he simply entered the small shack without preamble, looking for the Rougarou he had hired. Well, truth be told it was more of a conditional blackmail than a hiring of the creature. They were easy to manipulate and wouldn't reveal whomever or whatever took the woman under any circumstances. Therefore, Coyote's nefarious scheme would remain unknown to all except those whom Coyote chose to share the information with.

"Where is she?" Coyote asked as he looked around for the captured female he commissioned to have taken.

The creature with the body of a scaly human and the head of a wolf pointed to the back of the shack. Coyote went to look in the direction indicated to him. The box she was being held in was made of a plexiglass-like material which also acted as a one way viewing mirror. They could see and watch her but she could not see anything of where she was or who might be gazing upon her. The material was also sound proof, so she couldn't hear what was being said and have the opportunity to recognize possible voices.

When Coyote saw the female contained within, he was furious.

"What the fucking hell? You captured the wrong female! Who the fuck is this?" Coyote stopped his tirade and squinted closer at the captive, suddenly realizing who it was. He walked around the cage stroking his beard. This may be more advantageous after all. A better happenstance. Yes. This could actually work out better in the overall long run. She was coming of age, but still young and impressionable. If he played his cards just right, he could have an even greater advantage than he had originally anticipated. The only problem would be Mel. Coyote was going to have to plan this carefully. Very, very carefully.

Stepping back to the Rougarou, Coyote made all the necessary arrangements with the creature to transfer Trinity to a place which was not only secure, but also undetectable from Mel and the other gods. Then, he would have to go to work on the young daughter of the guardian.

Trinity looked up when the door opened. She wondered if she was finally going to see her kidnapper or maybe learn why she was taken. Maybe she could barter with them to release her. Her father was a god. Surely that would have some pull in her liberation from this prison she found herself in. Trinity had tried for the past few days to touch the minds of her parents, or even her brother: anyone in the hopes of them finding her. She just wanted to go home. Wanted to be in her room daydreaming about other realms. Only now, she had no interest in traveling anywhere unless her family took her.

A young man was brought in, his hands zip tied behind his back. He wasn't as old as her brother, but appeared to be only a year or two older than herself. Seventeen, maybe eighteen tops. He was very good looking. His hair was dark and curly, his eyes grey. His skin a slight olive tone. He had an athletic form and a purposeful gait, despite the bruises and cuts that appeared on his upper torso, arms and face.

Strong arms manhandled him, throwing him in and slamming the door shut, the locking mechanism audible as it was clicked back into place. The new male prisoner looked at her warily as he moved to the furthest opposite corner to sit down cross-legged on the floor, his head resting back against the bars of the cage. There was a small drape used to curtain-off a portion of the room in order to give each of them a bit of privacy when it became necessary, but otherwise the two cages occupied the small Spartan space.

Trinity gave him a skeptical look as she kept her eye on him. She wondered what they could possibly want with him. She hadn't recognized either of his handlers. She still didn't know where she was, why she was taken or who took her.

She watched as he wiggled, moving his secured wrists under his ass, down his thighs and over his feet to now be in front of him. He gnawed at the plastic tie keeping his wrists bound together. After a while, he finally was able to pull it apart using his strength to break the weakened restraints. Once having freed his appendages, he rubbed his wrists and flexed his fingers to regain circulation.

Trinity was intrigued at his fortitude. She had to admit he was the sweetest bit of man-candy she had ever seen, though her experience at seeing others who weren't hundreds or thousands of years older than herself were far and few between and could be counted on one hand. One finger even. She wasn't sure if she should talk to him or not. He seemed as wary of her as she was of him.

Once his hands were free, he stood and began pacing, testing the parameters of his cage, trying to find a weakness. He kept one eye on her as he did so, as if skeptical she was actually a prisoner and not in on his capture.

"Who are you?" he growled at her after pacing and examining the enclosure he was now confined in.

"Trinity," she answered simply. "You?"

"Nathan," he gruffly responded.

"Do you know who is doing this? Who has captured us? Or why?"

Nathan peered over at her as if she suddenly grew three heads. "You don't know?"

She shook her head. "No. I only know I was captured by some odd-looking creature with the head of a wolf and the scaly body of a biped reptile. I had never seen one before. I was rendered unconscious and when I came to, I was in this cage. I've seen or spoken to no one. The creature has brought me food, but other than that I have been alone."

"How long?"

She thought about it for a couple of minutes. "I'm not sure how long I was out, but I think I have been here for about a week. Maybe?"

Nathan gave one quick nod of acknowledgement then sat on the bed, crossing his arms across his broad chest.

Again, she asked him, her desperate need to know evident in her tone, "Do you know who took us? Or why? Is it for ransom? Please, tell me if you know."

Nathan frowned at her. "I don't know. Only one I saw was the Rougarou."

"Rougarou? Is that what the creature is?"

"Yes. Half wolf, half gator-man, lives in the swamplands. I know what he wants with me, but what he wants with you, I don't have a clue."

"What does he want with you?"

"He wants to know some information I have. But I won't tell him and I won't tell you. I will die first."

"I don't want to know whatever the information is. I don't know anything. I just want to go home," Trinity cried and turned away to put her back to him as she sat on her own bed.

Nathan was quiet for a few moments, watching her. "Hey. Trinity. Look. I'm sorry. I didn't mean anything by it. I'm sure you're scared. I am, too. We will get out of this. I swear. You have to just cooperate and, I bet, he will let you go back home soon. Maybe he is just waiting to get paid by your parents. Then you can be free. I don't know, but it will be okay."

"How can you promise that? You are stuck here too."

"Because you are not alone anymore. I am here. Besides, if they wanted to do you any harm, they already would have. You said you've been here for maybe a week. More than enough time to do something nasty if they were going to. Which means, you are valuable. If you don't know anything, then it's probably a ransom and as soon as the deal is made you can go home. Easy peasy."

"I hope you're right, Nathan. Gods, I hope you're right."

## Chapter 5

Logan wandered the swamps, sinking into the mud. At times, the mud reached his knees and others, his hips. The pungent order of decay permeated the air about him. After he and his parents searched for hours, they decided to split up and cover more ground. He watched his mother shift into a white wolf, trying to use her olfactory perception to uncover Trinity's scent. However, the land was too porous and the odors from the rotting vegetation too strong, covering any discernible redolence which might otherwise be detected.

As Clarissa sniffed around as best she could under the circumstances, Mel turned to his son, placing a hand on his arm to hold him back. He lowered her voice so the wolf would not hear them, even with her exceptional hearing.

"What are you hiding, Logan?"

Logan appeared surprised, then resigned and almost relieved. "I was going to mention it sooner, but, I wanted to be sure first." He didn't add Shara thought it best to keep the information from them for the time being.

Clarissa moved out of sight as she continued her search, leaving father and son the opportunity to talk in private as they walked.

"This isn't a time for caution, Logan. The life of your sister is at stake. Even if you don't think it important or consequential. Sometimes we are not the best judge of what information could be useful." Mel moved in such a way as to face Logan.

"Whatever secret you are keeping, I will not judge or scold you for it now."

Logan hesitated a moment more, checking to see if his mother was still nearby in case she might overhear them. "There is a woman who comes to the gardens every couple of weeks. Today was her day to come, but she told me the last time she was here, she would be running late and could not get away as easily as usual. She has always said no one could know she came to the garden, because her life would be in danger if anyone knew. She never said who was after her or why."

"Who is she? How long has she been visiting? Why does she come?"

"Her name is Jasmine, but I really don't know much about her. She came to see mother's roses, and then kept coming to visit them and me. She has been arriving in the garden for about ten years now."

"Ten years! You have been meeting this woman in the garden for ten years?"

Logan lowered his head, slightly ashamed it had gone on so long without them knowing. "Yes. Ten years. I was fourteen when I first saw her trying to find the entrance into our garden."

"And you have been meeting her there ever since." It was a statement not a question. Mel peered closely at his son, a penetrating look Logan had detested but knew it meant he was looking deep into the man's soul. "You are in love with her." Again, another statement.

Logan had not thought about it, but with the words there between them he could not refute it either. "Yes. I am."

Mel gave a solitary nod then turned back towards the way Clarissa had taken off.

"I suggest you don't let your mother know this at the moment. She will feel like she is losing you and she is already distraught over Trinity." He started walking again. "As for Jasmine, she may or may not be the reason Trinity was abducted. Regardless, she obviously needs someone to protect her as well if she has been fearful enough after all this time to still hide her identity from you or the reason she is being hunted. Whatever her secret might be, it deserves your attention. When we find your sister, you should consider finding a way to be with Jasmine."

Logan was stunned speechless for several moments. His father had always been fair and diplomatic when it came to his children, but he had not believed he could be this generous. Although both of his parents had been training him for several years, he had always assumed he would never be able to leave the Nether Realm except on excursions. Yet, now his father was telling him to go protect the woman he had cared deeply for.

Azamel seemed to understand his son's quietness. "When I fell in love with your mother, I was told we couldn't be together. It tore me up inside, but I did as I was commanded, because I had to. I don't want that for you. If you love someone, nothing should prevent you from being together.

However, son, do understand, you need to know about her and why she is running. You can't protect her if you don't know about her, no matter how much you love her. You need the knowledge to safeguard her appropriately, or you could lose her forever because you didn't have the adequate information you needed to assist her."

"When we find my sister, I will go to her, Dad. I will get all the answers to keep her safe."

Trinity looked up when the Rougarou came into the room, heading straight for Nathan's cage and Nathan himself. The young man tried to escape past the monster, but he was caught quickly and held immobile by the massive beast. Without a second thought, Nathan's throat was slit.

A scream resounded throughout the room and it was only her throat crying out in protest. She realized she was the one making the shrill sound. She stopped screaming by putting her hand over her mouth, trying desperately not to gag as the sanguine liquid flowed from the slice along his jugular. Trinity had never seen or experienced anything such as someone being killed in front of her. She had never seen anyone die and she felt so sickened by the act, as well as helpless. She was only sixteen, for gods' sake. Why would she be exposed to something like that? Why was she being exposed now?

She grabbed the bars in front of her. Her mouth opened again, but this time silent as she gaped in stunned surprised. She couldn't understand why the creature, the Rougarou, just killed Nathan. No word, no explanation, no remorse.

Had he outlived his usefulness? Had he given them what they wanted? Or did they realize he would never betray whatever secret he carried which they clamored for?

Over the past few weeks, she had come to know Nathan. They had developed a bond of sorts. Mutual prisoners who have come to share in the experience and supported the other. In truth, he calmed her fears more than she did for him. He was the one who reassured her when she cried at night, missing her family. He was the one who got her talking about life in the Nether Realm with her family. She was careful, or at least she hoped she was, in making sure there was no relevant confidential information disclosed during their conversations. She hoped nothing she said could be used against her or her family, although she had never been in such a situation before, nor away from home, so she had no clue if what she was saying was harmful to her family or not. She could only hope.

Seeing Nathan be murdered in front of her was, therefore, a huge shock as well as loss. Her only companion, her only friend in this predicament she had been forced into, was suddenly taken from her.

The Rougarou turned to her and gave Trinity an evil smirk. He was holding the blade aloft, dripping with blood. He stood facing her, holding the slumped body of the youthful man with the other hand, as if waiting for her to say something, enjoying her reactions. She didn't expect Nathan's eyes to suddenly snap open, immediately trying to regain his footing. She hadn't noticed moments prior: the blood flow had stopped and his wound had healed. So, Nathan was an immortal.

In one instant, she was happy, relieved Nathan would be okay. In the next, horrified as the Rougarou sliced his throat again, repeating the previous motion.

Trinity cried out, "No! No! Nathan! Stop it!"

Thrice more Nathan awoke momentarily, only to be immediately killed again and again. After the fifth time, the guard moved closer to her, dragging the still form of Nathan with him as if he were nothing more than a rag doll.

"Do you want this to end?"

"Yes. Gods, yes. Please, stop hurting him."

"Will you be willing to do anything to prevent his continued, repeated death?" As if to make his point, he sliced Nathan's throat just as he was becoming awake once more.

"Stop! Yes. Anything. Just stop. Please!" Trinity pleaded, her arms outstretched through the bars as if reaching for him to pull him to safety, despite that she was too far away to touch him.

Nodding, the wolfman snarled. "Know I'll continue doing this if you go back on your word."

"I won't. I promise. What do you want? Just tell me what you want from me to stop hurting him!"

The Rougarou came over, his jowls were dripping with saliva, his fangs bared. His elongated black snout glistened with Nathan's splattered blood.

"You will find it."

Trinity was baffled. "Find what?"

"What your mother protected and thought destroyed. Somewhere, a small spark exists. He feels it. Not often, not strongly, but it's there and with it, with just the small piece, he might find more. But even a small piece will be enough for him to succeed in his plans. He needs it and he needs you to find it."

"I have no idea who or what you are talking about. I don't know anything about what my mother might or might not have protected or what might or might not have been destroyed. Regardless, whatever it was or is, how would I even find it?"

True, Trinity knew how her parents met, same as her brother Logan, but like her sibling, she was unaware of what specifically her mother guarded. Regardless, Trinity wasn't about to let this creature assume she knew what her mother protected and give any indication in aiding him against her parents.

Nathan groaned as he opened his eyes. He was aware the Rougarou was still in his cage,

63

holding him by the back of his neck. Nathan struggled to get free and the swamp creature released him, the beast's attention on Trinity. Nathan quickly scrambled to the far corner, huddling quietly, listening as the two spoke. He didn't want to be noticed, didn't wish to die again. It hurt each and every time. His soul, his spirit, bounced back and forth between his body and the ethos like some fricking bungee cord snapping after being pulled taut.

Trinity noticed him hunkered in the farthest reaches of the cage, almost cowering in fear of being assaulted once again. She wished she could go to him, put her arms around him, hold him, but she also realized she was keeping the creature busy and something was better than nothing.

"You will be trained. It's inbred within your maternal line. It's your calling. You just need to know how to sense it and that can be learned."

"You make me sound like some dog sniffing out a scent. A bloodhound or something." Trinity blanched as she realized who and what she was talking to. The Rougarou snarled, pouncing towards the bars Trinity was still clinging to, causing her to jump back.

The Rougarou laughed. An eerie sound coming from a wolf's jowls.

"In a way, you're a bloodhound and you'll be used to find his desire."

"And when I've found it? What happens to me then? To Nathan?"

"That's not up to me. I follow orders just as you soon will."

With those final words, he jumped towards Nathan, causing the young man to jerk away, bouncing against the bars at his back and side, startled and frightened. Nathan cried out, cringing as the massive Rougarou grabbed his arm and propelled him out of the room.

Trinity yelled, "Stop! No! You promised!" However, they were out the door without another word to her.

Once in the hall and away from sight and sound of Trinity's prison, the Rougarou dropped his hand and lowered his head. "Did I do well, Master?" he asked in a reverent tone.

The form of Nathan shimmered and grew to that of a man. His shoulders became broader, his hips narrower. He was ripped, but lithe, wiry, yet strong. A mustache, beard and longer hair appeared on him, when only moments ago a youthful countenance existed. His voice also changed to a deeper resonance.

"You did very well, Axiso, my pet. Retire to your room. I shall meet you in a bit."

Coyote waited until the Rougarou left before heading to his office. There were a number of items he needed to prepare in order to train Trinity appropriately in finding the remnants of the Gem of Avarice.

## Chapter 6

It had been weeks when Clarissa finally returned wearily to the house and headed up to her room. She wanted to check on Zenthus but she desperately needed a shower and some fresh clothes. After the first few days, Mel, Logan and Clarissa had decided to split up to cover more ground. Maurepas was a gloomy area and, even though there was sunlight, there was such a dense covering of cypress trees and vines it cast a gloom everywhere.

She searched for her daughter, questioned every beast she could find in the swampland. Clarissa ignored the stings of the bugs which constantly attacked her as she turned over every rock and stone in hopes of finding some inkling of where Trinity had been taken. She didn't care how ruthless she was. Didn't care she was creating a terror in her own right, with the wake of broken Rougarous she'd left behind in her quest.

Clarissa may not have had the ability to go to the human world but she was able to go to other realms, and her powers still worked. She may be older, but she continued to train, first with Mel, then in preparation for Logan to protect himself. She had just started to train Trinity. Clarissa berated herself for not starting general protection moves with her daughter sooner. It might have helped. Instead, Clarissa had considered her daughter safe with years of time before she came of age to start training. She wanted to protect her, not have Trinity aware of a world where evil lurked, preying on the innocent. Clarissa didn't want Trinity to know of a place where someone would cause one so sweet and loving any kind of harm. Such a fool Clarissa was for thinking such a thing. She was such an idiot for believing she could protect her daughter from the evils of the universe.

Clarissa paused on the stairwell and hung her head, trying to overcome the feeling like being punched in the stomach so all the air left her lungs at the thought of her own foolishness at not training and protecting Trinity better. Clarissa had been stupidly naïve and she lost her family as a result. Why would she have thought Trinity would be even better shielded from the horrors and cruelty of the outside world, better than her parents and siblings were? Why couldn't she have realized not instructing Trinity was so detrimental to her daughter's preparedness for life? At least Clarissa's father tried to equip her when she was old enough to understand. Of course, she didn't have her powers yet, but her father made sure Clarissa was aware of some martial art techniques. She should have done the same for Trinity. Clarissa should have started teaching her from the moment she could stand and talk. Why? Why was she so blinded in not preparing her daughter better? Why did she think she had so much time she could waste it?

Pulling herself up, she continued to the room she shared with the demon judge and executioner. For the first time in a very long time she thought about the events of her family's demise.

Clarissa was the baby of the family and the only daughter to the twelve brothers born before her. As a result, her parents let her get away with a bit more than they did her siblings.

The morning had started like every other, busy with cooking, cleaning and the mild arguments of those waiting impatiently for other family members to get out of the bathroom. She pictured in her mind the face of her brother, Johann, as he was that day, looking nervous and anxious as he prepared to tell his family the news. He was her favorite brother, despite being overprotective, who teased her mercilessly but was still there for her with whatever she needed. Whatever she desired, he would make sure she got it. He loved her dearly and she him, more than words could say. However, that particular morning she got very angry with him, a regret which stayed with her for a very long time.

Johann had told his family he and his new wife, Marinka, were going to move out of the family home. Clarissa was shocked and railed on him. How could he leave her? Why did he have to go and leave their residence? Oh sure, it wasn't like he was departing the area they lived in, but still, they wouldn't be there when she got up, nor went to bed at night. Also, his wife said none of the family could visit at their new place. Marinka didn't like Clarissa's family much, especially her. Marinka felt Clarissa and Johann were just a bit too close for siblings, a bit too affectionate. To this day, Clarissa missed the feeling of him around and protecting her.

She missed the way he would tease her, tell her what to wear and whom she could associate with. Most of all, she missed their discussions about everything imaginable.

Johann had made the declaration to everyone that crisp, bright, cold day. He didn't even warn her alone, just announced to everyone they would be moving out at the end of the month. Family was only welcomed when they were specifically invited. Clarissa's heart broke as she ran from the table in tears at the very thought. Johann found her outside, weeping softly. She clung to him as he approached her and begged him not to go. What was she to do without him in her life? How could he be so selfish as to desert them and listen to his wife, leaving his family, tradition and worst of all, abandoning her?

She shook her head now at how foolish she was, how young and greedy for his time and attention she had been. She pushed him away, yelled at him. Johann had reached out to her, told her he would always be there, but she didn't listen. She didn't care what he had to say at that point. Her heart ached. She was going to make sure he knew it and hurt him, too. She could never take the words back that she had thrown at him so harshly that morning.

Had she known then it would be the last conversation she had with him, she would have said so many things differently. Who knew her life would change just moments later that day?

As she remembered the chronology of events which took place, she whispered, "I'm so sorry, brother. I need and love you terribly and I miss you so much. I never meant any of the words I said. I was rash and young. I never should have said I hated you more than life itself and wished you were dead, when it was the farthest thing from the truth."

Although she still could never undo the hurt she caused Johann as her last words rang in the still, cold, crisp air around them before she turned and ran off, she had since seen him to know all was forgiven.

As Clarissa stripped to head for the shower to wash up from the excursions into Maurepas Swamp, she thought about Johann. His last act was to save her as he sacrificed himself so she could get away.

There was nothing she wished she could undo more than those words she never, ever truly meant but instead were said in the heat of anger. How often had she replayed the day in her mind, trying to recall every little detail? Once Clarissa had run from the house, she hid in the woods for hours. Finally, she had calmed herself down enough to try and send a mental message to her family. She was still too upset at Johann and Marinka to see them at the moment but she wanted to go home. She tried to call out to her parents through her telepathy but there was no response. She had no idea what was happening, only a strong sense of unease settled around her, a desperation she needed to get back as quickly as possible. Why did no one answer her mental link?

Shifting into her wolf form, she began to run. She knew she was faster in this guise and her gut instincts told her she needed to get there as quickly as she could. She wanted to crawl into her papa's lap and have Mama chastise Johann for his announcement earlier. Why weren't her parents responding to her either? Why were they ignoring her mental calls? Was she maybe linking them incorrectly? Could werewolves send a message to the wrong head or get busy signals? She had never heard of such a thing but, then again, she really didn't know for sure.

One more bend and she would be home. She shifted back to her natural human form; a coat wrapped tightly around her body as soon as she was able to materialize clothes on her otherwise naked figure.

She rounded the corner and came to a dead stop. She blinked, unsure she was actually seeing reality. The snow in the road was blood red as bodies were strewn about. Intermingled with the still figures of her young nieces and nephews were the bodies of wolves, their throats cut or their guts torn out and laid next to their bodies in a bloody pile matted with their fur. She was sickened and shocked by the sight. Tears streamed down her face as she ran, continuing to look for other members of her family. Surely they would be safe. It was important they were okay. They were her parents and her brothers. They just *had* to be alright.

She burst into the house; her brothers, more nephews and nieces, slaughtered, the floorboards forever stained with their sanguine liquid. She screamed in horror and in agony. Hearing some scuffling and other noises, she ran towards the sound which led her to the back yard. Once there, she saw her brothers Johann and Sebastian fighting five wolves. She stared in horror as the wolves took down Sebastian, tearing him to shreds with their teeth and claws, and he soon lay unmoving at Johann's feet.

Johann saw her and she heard his desperate plea in her head. *'Take my bike and run away.* Never *come back. Run and live!'*

Wasting no more time, she ran to the shed where the motorcycle was kept. Just before she turned away from the grisly scene, she noticed Johann give her a very subtle nod, spin and run in the opposite direction. Johann knew full well the wolves would chase him and hopefully not notice her attempted bolt for freedom.

Johann swung at the wolves who were attacking him, trying desperately to keep them occupied so Clarissa could escape. She backed up slowly, wanting to flee the nightmare and not gain their attackers' attentions, but it was too late. One of the wolves smelled her fear on the wind and turned towards her direction. Snarling, his fangs dripping with saliva and blood, he charged at her. She skidded slightly and then ran as fast as her feet would carry her.

Clarissa entered the shed where there was a brand new red Ducati, which her brother Johann had brought home a week prior. He had taken her for a ride just days before and showed her how to drive it. Johann had held her while she tried to maintain balance and encouraged her to keep trying until she was successful.

She ran to the parked motorcycle but felt the heavy paws of a wolf pouncing on her back, pushing her forward as her face quickly met the floor of the building. The wolf's fangs sank into her shoulder. She felt the sinewy muscles and tissue being torn as she screamed and kicked, tears overflowing down her already dampened cheeks. Her hands reached out, trying to find anything to dislodge him off of her. She found a crowbar and her fingers stretched and tried to roll it towards her for a better grip. It was just out of reach and kept rolling back slightly. Finally, after several attempts, she was able to grasp it. Getting a good hold on the crowbar, she twisted at her waist and whacked the wolf in the head with as much strength as she could muster. Clarissa repeatedly hit the wolf until the vise on her shoulder slackened. She squirmed out from under his heavy body and quickly got on her feet. Her one arm hung slightly limp from the shoulder wound, she found it hurt to move it. Blood, *her* blood, dripped down her arm. As the wolf staggered towards her, she growled and kicked him.

Her father had made sure his children knew how to defend themselves. She always thought carving wood with him was more fun than practicing kicks and hits but she was never more thankful he had encouraged she learn.

Once the wolf was back far enough, he took a running leap at her again. This time she caught the beast in the chest with the pointy end of the crowbar, using the metal rod to flip the wolf alongside of her, unmoving other than a twitch or two as he expelled his last breath. She sank to her knees as she let go of the bloodied instrument. Having taken the life of a living creature, she felt she should be remorseful but she wasn't. That creature helped to kill everything she loved. Everything which made up her life was now all gone. Shakily regaining her feet, she ran to the bike, rolled it out and revved it up. Jumping on it, she sped as fast as she could to get away. A few wolves tried to chase her. A couple of them even materialized in front of her but she skirted around them and kept driving, never looking back as she knew she couldn't afford to. She was blinded mostly by the tears that streamed down her face, but she did not stop. She just kept moving with as much speed as she could and prayed they wouldn't find her. Yet, a part of her hoped they would catch her so they could kill her also and she would once again be with her loved ones. Her life was destroyed in a matter of minutes.

She never thought in her wildest dreams she would have the chance to see her family again, even if only for a few swift moments. It was enough, though, for her to apologize and beg forgiveness of her brother, Johann. It was the time she needed to make sure he knew she never meant those last words she spat at him. She had walked among her family, clearing the air, so to speak, of the ills which haunted her throughout the days following their demise.

Mel had seen how her anger at the world for her family's loss, of being alone and given a responsibility she was ill-prepared for, took its toll on her. He realized she needed to control her anger, her feelings derived from the murders of her family. Her enemies would use it against her and to their own benefit. He trained Clarissa, not to fight but to forgive herself and to love again. Mel didn't need to teach her to fight. Her skill was excellent as is.

So why, she wondered as she stepped into the shower to wash off the grime of the swamps, why had she not done the same for her own daughter? If she had taught Trinity how to fight, how to protect herself, maybe her youngest child would not be missing.

Clarissa washed and dried herself before slipping on a pair of pajamas. She couldn't remember the last time she was this exhausted and hated she had to stop looking in order to get some rest. Truth was, she had been searching non-stop for over a week with no results and little food or sleep in the process. However, every minute she was not out there looking was another minute her daughter wasn't home, so Clarissa continued to press on until exhaustion overcame her and she finally returned to recharge her batteries.

Clarissa pulled the covers back and was about to crawl into bed when the door opened and Mel walked in. The smile Clarissa gave him instantly disappeared as she saw his countenance. Rushing to his side, she grasped his arm in fear.

"You found her? She is not, I mean, she is okay? Please, tell me she is okay."

Tears sprang to her eyes as she waited for Mel to speak. He didn't say anything for several minutes, peering down into those green orbs he fell so deeply in love with. When he did speak, it was nothing what she thought he would say.

"How dare you?" he growled low, trying to maintain a calm he did not feel.

Clarissa peered at him, totally perplexed. "How dare I what? Search for my daughter?"

"I expect you to search, but not to abuse innocent creatures in your questioning."

Now she understood. He was upset because she used some heavy handed tactics with her questioning in order to get the truth of who had taken Trinity. Anger flared inside of her, her emerald eyes darkening.

"I did what I had to do in order to try and find answers. In order to find Trinity."

"I agree with doing everything possible to find her, but not beating up the Rougarou. Not all of them are guilty or know anything, and breaking their arms and legs, sending fireballs as warning shots and stabbing them in the shoulders or thighs, is not the way to get the answers you are seeking. Worse, you are creating an atmosphere which is becoming rapidly volatile. I've never had issues with this race before, but I am not going to be able to keep the peace with them if you keep up your severe oppressive approaches to your investigation."

"So what? Am I supposed to pour them tea and serve them crumpets in hopes they will just fork the information over? Do you think there is time for that? Every minute they don't answer is one more minute Trinity is not where she belongs. Here! It's one more minute she is gods knows where and in danger. One more minute for whomever took her to do horrible things to her."

Clarissa gripped the lapels of the black suit jacket he was wearing. Azamel looked fresh and clean. He must have been home for a while, but she couldn't think about how sexy he looked or how good he smelled. His accusations infuriated her. On top of her concern for Trinity, she was furious with him.

"I will do whatever it takes to get the information needed to find her. I'm sorry if that goes against your diplomatic plans with the swamp creatures, but I am not sorry about my methods of trying to find her. She is my daughter. I will do whatever it takes to get her back."

She released her hold on him, pushing him back and away from her. Spinning, she turned her back to him, trying to catch her breath, trying to calm down. She didn't have much of a chance before he grabbed her upper arm and spun her around to face him. He pressed his face close to hers. Had he not been so angry, she would almost think he was about to kiss her. His warm breath blew against her face as he struggled to keep some semblance of calm in order to talk to her without yelling.

"I have to be diplomatic. They have not done anything as a race to incur my wrath. I will not blame a whole ethnicity for the actions of a few." Mel let Clarissa go, running a hand through his hair in frustration.

"I will do everything I can to find her. I am not blaming all of them for taking her, but I refuse to leave any stone unturned in my search. Don't you care? Aren't you willing to do anything to find our daughter?"

"Of course. Fuck! Do you think I am pussy-footing around in my attempt to find her? But I am not going to start a war to locate her either. Wasn't it you who taught me years ago that I could catch more flies with honey and not vinegar? Maybe you should take your own advice."

"My own advice? Thanks for throwing those words back at me. My own advice was getting me nowhere. My own advice had them ignoring me like I was invisible or non-existent. My own advice wasn't getting me any results."

"And is treating them all like enemies obtaining any results in finding her? No! All it is doing is banding them against us instead of making them willing to help us."

Mel started pacing about the room, his hands flinging wildly as he talked. "You think I am not doing everything possible to find her? She is my daughter, too. I won't abandon her or the search to find her, but I can't afford a war with a species I have never had prior issues with. I don't know why she was taken, or by whom. I have a feeling a couple of the Rougarou were hired to capture her, but since there has been no ransom, I am not sure for what nefarious purpose they plan to use her to their advantage. Zenthus and Jakome killed the attackers, with the exception of the one who took her. Rougarou are solitary creatures for the most part. Small packs at best. They don't like to talk and share. None know or will know unless they were a part of the scheme, and I think those that were are now spending their time in their version of hell."

Azamel turned back to look at Clarissa, a softening of his features coming over him slightly. "I'm trying to talk to Chip to let me into his land to find their souls and talk to them, but he says he can't do that. Or he won't. Even Nana cannot force him." He stood in front of her again, peering down into those eyes he loved so much. "I'm not giving up, Rissa. I just don't need a fucking war on top of this too."

"I'm not stopping. If breaking a few arms or setting fire to a couple of legs is going to get the information I need, then the possibility of a war would be worth it. I need to find her," Clarissa railed on him. "I won't leave her alone, at the hands of whoever has her, and hope they are merciful. I need to find her. I *have* to find her!"

She began to beat against his chest with each of her declarations. After the last one, she collapsed against him, her fists still against his broad chest, her head between her hands. For the first time since Trinity had been taken, she broke down and wept, the emotions finally overwhelming her to such a degree she could do no less. Mel had broken the wall of detachment she had built to focus on getting Trinity back. Azamel wrapped his arms about her, holding her close in his embrace, his cheek resting against the top of her head. He rubbed her back softly, trying to give her the comfort he knew she needed but would never ask for. She was too stubborn and proud. She always had been from the moment he first met her. He knew this was tearing her apart. Hell, it was ripping out his insides as well, but he had to be strong for his family, for his wife. And he made a silent promise to her, to himself. When he found Trinity and she was safely home, he would make sure whoever took her would pay the price for their hubris in a long and suffering kind of way. Nothing in any realm would stop him from exacting his revenge for the heartbreak and worry they brought to his family and himself.

He could feel Destruction calling to be released, but with nowhere specific to go, it was too dangerous to give the demon his head to freely destroy the realm. Destruction was perfect for exacting retribution or protection, but for searching? Not so much.

## Chapter 7

Months had passed and Azamel and Logan branched into other realms in search of Trinity. Shara stayed at the house to help Zenthus recover and handle all inquiries as to where the family was. She also fielded any supposed sightings and passed them along to Mel to be investigated in hopes of locating his daughter. Nothing panned out. Clarissa remained in the Maurepas Realm since it was the natural home of the Rougarou. Still, none of their searches had produced results. It was almost as if Trinity had been wiped from existence.

Logan stood facing the black roses in the garden. They were beginning to get a bit wild without the constant trimming and tending from his mother, who has been so preoccupied of late in the frantic search for Trinity. As each day passed, so her desperation grew. He had seen her but only a few times since Trinity had been taken from this very garden. When he had seen her, his mother had been haggard from being so distraught. Dark circles under her eyes from lack of sleep. Loss of weight from lack of eating. She appeared more wearied than he had ever seen her, although he couldn't blame her in the least.

Azamel also appeared exhausted and worn down, yet every day they were out there searching. Every day they hoped for a clue, a lead, something which would let them know where their youngest child was located. Every day they clutched to the belief they would find Trinity and return her to the safety of the manor. Yet, every night they returned disappointed in their failure to discover where she was or who might have taken her.

As he stood there, he felt a presence enter the garden and turned to face her. A smile appearing on his own worn face. It was the first time he had seen her in months. They had been so busy searching for his sister, he had done or concerned himself with little else. Even her. He moved quickly to be by her side, pulling her into his arms.

"Jasmine! I was worried about you. I didn't know how to find you. Are you okay?"

"I'm sorry, Logan. I heard about your sister, Trinity. I felt it best to stay hidden longer. The ripple effects of Trinity's abduction have rebounded throughout the universes. My mother has kept me concealed. She also thinks Trinity was taken because of me, though she also believes Trinity will be used to hunt me. My mother is unaware I've ever come here or even that I am here now, but I had to see you. I have missed you so much."

"Why are you being hunted, Jaz? Why can't you tell me? I want to protect you, help to keep you safe, but I can't do that if I don't know what I am up against or why."

Jasmine pulled back within the confines of his arms. "How would you be able to do that anyways when you are stuck here?"

"I'm not. I can go into the human world to guard you. My parents have trained me well. We have searched for months with no sign of my sister and my father feels I should not give up my entire life. I can still hunt for her, but he feels I should be there to protect you. He knows how I feel about you."

"You told him?" She was astounded, and suddenly nervous about others, especially the demon judge, knowing about her or that she was even here, much less visiting here for the past decade.

"He suspected something when we first started looking for Trin. He asked and I had to tell him the truth. He didn't mind, though. I was rather surprised. He wanted me to be with you and help to keep you safe."

"And your mother?"

"She still doesn't know. Dad thought it was best she not have to worry about me while she is still so distraught over my sister. She is going to be upset as it is, when she learns I am leaving to live in the human world so I can be with you, before finding Trinity. She feels like she has lost one child as it is, to have me leave so soon will only agitate her further."

Jasmine frowned. She hadn't really been living in the Human Realm. Yet, this was not the time or place to discuss all of this.

"When will you be going to the Human Realm? When will you tell your mother?"

"As soon as I can. I wanted to talk to you first. I don't know where you live or where I am going. I, honestly, wasn't even sure you would want me."

"Yes. I want you," she said softly, looking up into those turquoise eyes she was so enamored with. "But you should know, I only live in the human world for short amounts of time. If I am there too long, I can be discovered."

"Who is hunting you? Why? What am I going to be up against?"

"It's a very long story and I will explain it all in good time. I promise." She pulled back and looked around nervously. "I need to go. I am being summoned. Meet me in New Orleans in one week. Bourbon Street, the Cat's Meow courtyard at midnight. I'll explain everything then." Jasmine leaned in and kissed his lips softly. "I promise. I'll tell you all about my strange life then."

"I will see you there at the appointed time. I will wait for you to tell me the whole kit and caboodle when we are together next." Logan paused then took a deep breath. "I know I have never said it, but I want you to know, Jaz, I have fallen in love with you."

Jasmine cupped his cheek and kissed him again. "I know." She then disappeared from his arms and he was left standing alone in a fragrant garden of black roses.

Jasmine entered the small cottage in Faefardom, the realm of the fairies, which resembled a building the Flintstones could've been perfectly content to have lived in. It was about the only realm protected from detection, thereby keeping her safe from being discovered. Her grandmother, Archanidou, was waiting for her. Although normally such a visit would not cause an issue, the fact her grandmother was here waiting for her could be a concern. She realized her presence would not have been detected since she was in another realm and they would have realized she had left the sanctity of Faefardom.

"You were in the Nether Realm again, weren't you, my child," Archanidou stated without preamble.

Jasmine flushed. She should have known she couldn't keep secrets from her grandmother. She wondered how long the woman had known. Archanidou answered the unspoken question as if she actually had said it aloud.

"I've only recently been made aware of your visits." Archanidou, also known as Spiderwoman, pointed to the seat next to her. "I've seen Azamel and I have seen the toll it has taken on him to have lost his daughter. I can't even imagine what Clarissa is going through. However, I take it they are not the ones you have concerned yourself with."

"No, Nunohum." Nunohum was the Native word for grandmother. "I went to see their son, Logan."

"A good looking male. If I was younger, I might have gone after him myself. Alas, I am too old for the likes of him. He takes after his father more in looks, but has his mother's kind heart and soul. He has the strength of both. I guess it has come time to let you go and live your own life. To be with him."

"Is it safe? Someone took Trinity. Someone could still be after me."

"It will never be safe for you, my child. You carry tainted blood inside which will always call to others. Sadly, it is not your doing but that of your mother's, gods above rest her soul on the Happy Hunting Grounds."

Jasmine knew the story. Had been given the knowledge of what power she held within and why others would always search for her. A stone once protected by the guardian, previously known as Clarissa, was destroyed in a dispute of the gods before Logan and her were even born. Archanidou sent her children to remove all the fragments of the crushed, broken gem to hide away. Jasmine's mother took her entrusted small remnant to the land of the Faes. She buried it with her eggs, knowing she could protect it best there. One egg somehow developed around the sliver of gem that remained and became infused inside the life source, which grew within.

Time moves slower in the land of the Faes than in the human or Nether Realms. When Jasmine was born, her body absorbed the particle that remained by the egg. It became part of her bloodstream, part of her life force. As soon as Jasmine opened her eyes, the stone's deep rich color, and a minute sense of the power, was discernable, giving off an orange-red color never seen before. Jasmine's mother died shortly after her birth. Archanidou realized the specialness of Jasmine so she kept her in Faefardom in order to conceal her from those who would seek her out in order to obtain the power which flowed within her very veins.

Spiderwoman made Jasmine very aware that Clarissa, having been the guardian tied to the Gem of Avarice, would sense it within her immediately if the two ever met. Trinity, as the female descendant of the keeper of the stone, would also sense it, even if she was not trained. The gem would call to all who were commissioned with the duty to prevent it from falling into the wrong hands. The only conclusion she could safely make was Trinity had been taken to try and locate Jasmine.

"I know, Nunohum, but how long do I keep hiding here? Somehow, someone sensed me and yes, maybe it was my own fault in doing so because I have left the safety of this realm, but I don't fit here. I don't belong here. The fairies have never accepted me, barely tolerated me."

Spiderwoman reached over and took Jasmine's hand in her own. "I know growing up here where you had few friends and only me as family was difficult for you. The Fae are not used to our kind. If you don't have wings then you can't soar with them, and that they find useless. As a result, you have been alone most of your life. I do not blame you for exploring away from this realm to find others just to talk to. However, you have been exposed. Nothing will change that. Nothing can reverse the knowledge you exist. Now, you can only prepare to face the challenge which awaits you as a result. If Logan is willing to be by your side to aid in keeping you from harm, I will rest easier knowing you have the comfort of another trained in defense. One who must care for you, for I can see within you the light you have for him and I cannot believe it would not be reciprocated.

"No more hiding, my child. It is time you live in the light and deal head-on the threat which has been looming since before you were born."

Archanidou pulled two dream catchers from beneath her shawl. One was in the form of a necklace to be worn around Jasmine's neck, the other a larger piece to be hung over her bed as she slept, wherever that may be. As Spiderwoman handed them to her granddaughter, she explained their powers.

"The one for your bed will protect you while you sleep, catching in its web all tendrils trying to locate where the miniscule sliver of stone still exists. You will have peace as you rest. The necklace, wear it at all times. It should block any who try to sense you, no matter the realm you are in. But, do not let the sunlight hit it, for it will absorb the sun and nullify the powers of the necklace. It will take the light of a moon to recharge it again. I cannot stop you from venturing forth, but I will be around should you need me. All you ever have to do is call to me and I shall be there as soon as I am able.

"I love you, my granddaughter. I always have and I always will."

"And I, you, Nunohum. Always and forever, you have my love."

Jasmine leaned over, hugging her grandmother tight. Realizing what she had to do, she then stood and went to pack what few items she possessed.

## Chapter 8

Logan walked the streets of New Orleans looking for the Cat's Meow. He had only arrived in the city a day before and was still getting acquainted with finding his way around. His mother had been none too pleased he was leaving for the Human Realm, even though she herself had instructed him to go. Of course, she told him before Trinity had been taken; before she lost her daughter to the unknown. Now, her son was leaving and, although she would know where he was, he wouldn't be with her, he wouldn't be under her protection or the sanctuary of the manor. He knew she was upset. He knew she didn't know about Jasmine or that his father had told him to go and protect the woman he had fallen in love with.

Logan tried to explain he would not give up searching for Trinity. He would keep looking, but it wasn't going to consume every moment of every waking hour for him like it had for her. If he wanted to make his mother angry, he certainly succeeded with those words. He felt awful he had hurt her like that. She was a good woman, a loving mother, and she didn't deserve such unkind words. He had not seen her when he left. He would apologize to her the next time he saw her. When he found a place, he would invite her to visit and offer to let her add the woman's touch she always bragged about whenever she re-decorated the manor.

As he walked down Bourbon Street, he saw the building just up ahead and quickened his pace. It stood on the corner, an opening within the wall facing Bourbon and St. Peter Streets could have originally been a door. It was half-walled with a wooden section reaching up to the back part of the stage, which contained a wildly painted piano. The other half-level opened so passersby could peer in at the show going on inside. A couple of women were on the stage singing some song he was unfamiliar with. They appeared pretty intoxicated and didn't seem to care how off-key they were, but were having a good time and getting the crowd worked up regardless. He headed past the open corner to a narrow door guarded by a big male wearing a Cat's Meow polo shirt and checking IDs as people walked in. His father had made sure he had all the proper identification materials he would need to live in this world, so he pulled his wallet out from his back pocket and removed the state identification card from within, showing it to the man who let him pass. Once inside he looked around quickly, trying to find access to the courtyard. It was not difficult to find as the place was not very big and the courtyard opening was just opposite the door from where he entered. Logan headed straight for it.

Another bar, entrance to the restrooms, a staircase leading upstairs and a couple of tables to stand or sit at were located in the small brick courtyard of the establishment. She was not there yet and he was slightly disappointed. He headed to the bar and ordered a beer, bringing it back to the table facing the two entrances from within the building.

Taking a sip from his beer, he played with the label. He was almost afraid she wouldn't show, even though he berated himself for being ridiculous in the process. He kept looking at his time piece and then at the doors any time he heard someone approach, only to be disappointed as it was someone heading to the restrooms behind him or up the staircase to the second floor and outside balcony which overlooked Bourbon Street.

Logan had lined up five bottles of empty beers and was about to give up when he heard a couple approach. He glanced up, although he was sure it wasn't her, only to see her with another man who was holding her hand. His heart sank immediately at the closeness of the couple. He thought she loved him and seeing her with another was like a slap in the face. Why did she ask to meet him if she was with someone else? How could she break his heart so easily?

The male led Jasmine to the only table occupied. He was only a little taller than Jasmine. Logan guessed about five foot ten inches, maybe eleven tops. He was lithe, athletic, even a bit wiry. He seemed very graceful and almost floated into the yard towards him. Did he catch a glimpse of gossamer wings on his back or had the five beers taken a bit of a hold on him?

Jasmine let go of the man's hand and hugged Logan, surprised when he didn't respond, only continued to glare at the male. Stepping back, Jasmine smiled, trying to ease Logan's obviously hurt emotions.

"I'm so glad you came, Logan. I apologize for being late but Tyler is not one for punctuality. Tyler, this is Logan." She said the latter name almost reverently and Logan had to look at her in astonishment at such softness. The look of adoration as she gazed upon him loosened him up slightly. He held his hand out to Tyler.

"Nice to meet you." Logan wanted to ask a myriad of questions, such as who was he, how long have you known him, what is he to you, but nothing came out.

Tyler gripped his hand and shook it. "Likewise. I have heard nothing but talk of you, Logan. I half expected to see you walking on water when we arrived since all she talks about ie you."

Jasmine slugged his arm. "Stop it," she teased lightly then turned back to Logan. "Tyler is like my guardian and my brother all rolled into one. He has appointed himself my protector for the most part, and although I find him overbearing and annoying most days, he is one of my best friends. He has helped to keep me sane when everything else failed." She plopped on the stool next to Logan, giving a quick glance at the beer bottles piled up before them. "I have made you wait a long time. I am so very sorry."

Tyler scooped up the empty bottles and grinned like the Cheshire Cat. "I'll buy the next couple of rounds. My apology for keeping you waiting so long." Tyler moved to the bar and placed the empties on it, ordering a round of beers for the three of them. He told the bartender to take his time in getting them, wanting to give Logan and Jasmine a moment to talk with as much privacy as a small area such as they were in could afford.

Logan still said nothing, just watched as Tyler walked away. Jasmine laid her hand on his, catching his full attention. "I really am sorry we were late. I wanted you to meet Tyler. He has covered for me a couple of times in order to see you over the years. He is such a dear friend to me. I hope he will be the same for you, if you give him a chance."

Logan softened at her touch and more so at her words. He didn't want to admit he was jealous when he first saw them together, hand in hand. Then her next words bothered him.

"When I moved to New Orleans, Tyler got us a place just outside of the French Quarter."

"You two *live* together?"

"Not like how you are making it sound, but yes. We share a place. It's warded and I am safe there. I only moved here a few days ago. Tyler learned I was coming and refused to let me be alone. He is a trained soldier and has assigned himself as my warden. Tyler got us a cottage and used some spells so I couldn't be easily found."

"Protected from what? What has hunted you all this time? What does it want?"

"It wants me. It wants my blood." She looked back at Tyler, who was starting to come over with the new round of beers, placing them on the table and taking a stool himself.

"Haven't you told him anything about what you are, Jazzy?" Tyler asked, almost amused.

"I didn't want to get him in trouble. And you know Nunohum, she would've had a fit if she thought I was telling everyone who and what I am."

Logan sat patiently, unsure what to make of the dynamics between the two of them.

Jasmine sighed and turned her full attention on Logan. "My grandmother is Archanidou. You might know her as Spiderwoman. I know she has visited your family often." She waited until that bit of news sank in before she continued.

Logan was taken aback. Spiderwoman had hundreds of children, but he never really gave much more thought about it than that, so to hear Jaz was related was indeed a surprise. After a few moments to absorb the information he voiced his bewilderment.

"So? What difference does that make?" Logan was unsure where this was going.

"None really, except knowing that I am descended from a god, just like you."

"Tell him the rest, Jazzy."

"I am, Ty, I am. Geez Louise, keep your lace panties on." She scolded Tyler then continued to Logan, "My mother was one of those sent to help your mother remove the shattered remnants of the stone your mother was assigned to guard. The sliver my mother was commissioned to hide, she took to Faefardom and buried with her eggs. Somehow, the power of the gem infused my embryo. It's in my blood. It courses through me. Something out there can feel it on occasion. If it finds me, it might try to take my blood to extract the powers the stone provides. Even such a small amount might be the key to tipping the scales of good and evil. And most likely, it will kill me in the process."

Logan was stunned. Not sure what else to do, he lifted his bottle and drained the entire thing down his throat. The idea the gem his mother guarded was now infused inside of Jasmine took a bit of time to comprehend, as well as all the implications of what it meant if she was found.

"That's why where you live is warded. To help hide its power flowing within you."

"Yes. Tyler is from that realm, too. He has powers to help hide his own differences among the mundanes of this world. He warded the building he bought so he could be in his natural state when he chooses without fear of detection. Because of the shielding on the building, it hides what flows inside me as well, just as the realm hid me from anyone not within the world itself. You know how precautionary and defensive the fairies are about the land they live in."

"Yeah. I have heard that. Which is why they don't allow many, if any, visitors to their realm."

"We are very solicitous of ours. And Jazzy is considered one of ours. So, I make sure she is safe-guarded." Tyler leaned in as if making a point to Logan, who only smirked back. The male did not make him worried in the least. After all, Logan was the son of the demon judge and executioner, as well as a kick-ass werewolf. A fairy wasn't about to scare him in the least.

Ignoring Tyler as well, Jasmine leaned closer to Logan. "Where are you staying?"

"Right now, in the Hotel Monteleone, but only until I find a more suitable apartment."

Jasmine gave a quick glance over at Tyler before turning back to Logan. "Stay with us. The Creole Cottage is not huge, but there are four bedrooms, living room, and kitchen. And, if you don't like being there, you can stay there until you find a place more suitable."

Again Logan looked astonished. There were a number of revelations happening tonight and none of them he prepared for or expected. He looked over at Tyler and seemed slightly uncomfortable at the idea of sharing a place with them. However, it would mean he was much closer to Jasmine and that made it a very promising idea. No fear of being together, of her being caught in his mother's garden, or of them really getting to know each other. Plus, Mel did tell him to guard her. What better way than to coexist in the same residence?

"That sounds like a pretty good plan," Logan admitted.

"Great. Come on then. Let's get you checked out of the hotel and moved into the cottage." Jasmine slipped off the stool and slipped her arm into Logan's as they began to walk out of the bar and down the street towards the Hotel Monteleone.

Tyler frowned. He wasn't too keen on the idea of Logan living with them. He realized part of it was because of the uneasy truce between Demonkin and Fae he had heard about his entire life. Some inbred inhibitions took a bit of time to overcome. He had a feeling this was going to be one of them. Tyler followed the couple to the hotel, warily watching others who passed, and kept an eye out for any trouble they might encounter. As Jazzy stated, he was a soldier before he took the assignment to make sure she was secure in the world of the humans.

Tyler had been trained to fight and defend almost from the moment of his birth. He was considered one of the most proficient warriors of the Fae. When the opportunity to become a personal bodyguard to Jaz arose, he quickly applied for the honor. He wanted the chance to actually do something with his unique set of abilities besides simply honing them with the rare possibility of actually putting them to use.

Despite all of Jasmine's talk about Logan, Tyler still hadn't fully decided if he was friend or foe. He would have to be very wary and see how it all played out.

## Chapter 9

Trinity was dragged from her cell to a solid white room and shoved inside. The room was stark and bare, with a chair and a fireplace with mantle. She looked around. No windows, no other doors but the one she was brought in from. A voice, hollow, rough and deep, almost mechanical, boomed throughout the room.

"Sit."

Trinity ignored the voice and instead tried the door. It was locked and she heard the Rougarou growl just on the other side.

"Sit!"

This time, she did as the voice commanded.

"Close your eyes."

Again, she hesitated.

"Do not make me keep asking you more than once." The disembodied voice boomed around her. "Or do I need to make an example of Nathan again?"

"No! I'm sorry. I'll do as you ask." Quickly, Trinity shut her eyes and waited for the next order.

"Empty your mind. Feel what is around you. Sense the very air that is in the room. Tell me what you smell. What you sense might have been in there."

Taking a deep breath, she emptied her mind and tried to use her senses as to what else might have been in that room. First she smelled food. A roasted turkey. Then she smelled something stronger. An almost unpleasant odor, like gym socks that had been stored in a locker for over a month with the corpse of a fish. The scent became stronger and she started to cough, then choke, finally opening her eyes as the expectorating became worse.

After coughing for several minutes, she finally settled down.

"What did you sense?" the voice asked.

"At first, turkey," she responded, wishing she had a glass of water to help the dry roughness which now coated her tonsils. "Then what smelled hideous. Like old socks and decaying fish guts."

"Good. There is water on the mantle."

She looked over at the once empty mantle only to see a pitcher of water and a glass. She rushed over to pour herself a glass only to drain it quickly and repeat the process. She slowed down after her second glass, sipping sporadically on her third.

Coyote thought about what she sensed. She had a really good start in her training. The turkey was the most recent. The decaying fish smell would have been the meeting he had in that room seven months ago with the Dafitca Demons. Their body odor was offensive to his sensitive sense of smell and he always had to have the room deodorized and sanitized whenever they came to meet with him. However, going to see them on their own turf was worse. At least here it was confined to just the one room.

He gave Trinity a few moments to adjust after their first attempt. Now he was ready to get back to work.

"Return to your seat." the voice boomed within the room, still mechanically disguised. Coyote would take every precaution to make sure she didn't know who was keeping and ordering her. "Close your eyes. This time I want you to focus not on smells, but on power. Not in the room, but in the air, the world around you."

"I'm not sure I can do that."

"You will try and you will keep trying to reach out with your mind. In time you will succeed."

"What am I looking for? How will I know if I found it?"

"You will know the answer to both when the time comes."

Trinity sat back, setting the water on the floor by her chair. She wished she had an inkling of what was going on. She could only hope she would help him find whatever he was looking for and quickly so she could go home. Her family must be freaking out over her being gone. She would probably be punished severely for leaving the manor and being captured. On second thought, maybe going home would not be such a good idea. She shook that thought out of her head immediately. No. Home, even if she was grounded for a century, would be better than being held here. The only thing that made this whole thing even bearable was meeting Nathan.

The young man was so kind and sweet. He made her feel comfortable and, even though they had only had their fingertips touch through the bars of their prison, she felt close to him. Truth be told, she had a crush on him and could see them as very good friends, maybe even more if they both survived this. She would make sure they both survived. She had to.

Closing her eyes, she concentrated, searching for a residue of power, an energy in the cosmos which called to her. She let her mind go, swimming around as if floating on a cloud, drifting from one place to another. Strong smells of leather, of gold, of money and greed would touch upon her briefly before moving away to make room for something else. She tried to find her parents, or even her brother, but every time she forced herself to find them, she felt a deep throbbing in her temple and had to pull back. She came to the conclusion she was being prevented from contacting anyone she knew. After the fifth attempt, she gave up and focused on what she was told to search for.

She had no concept of time. It seemed like hours she sat in the chair in the white room, her mind floating from one space to another. Coyote watched her and the walls around her. The room was specially warded. Glowing symbols would appear on the walls whenever she touched something with her mind. When she tried to focus on her family, her friends, a symbol would illuminate and darken in pulsing throbs which reminded Coyote of a heartbeat, until she backed off and moved to something else. He had to give her credit though, she was persistent. He counted five times she tried to reach the minds of her loved ones. Ten hours later, he felt it was enough attempts for one day. He sent Axios into the room and had her returned to her cell.

Each day they would repeat the process. Weeks passed. Months. Still, nothing called to her that he was looking for. The glyphs on the wall to notify him she succeeded, failed to shimmer awake with her success in contacting the piece of stone somewhere in the world. Maybe she was useless after all. Maybe he should send her home or feed her to the Dafitca Demons so there would never be any trace of her found. However, the Demons liked to talk and he didn't need word coming back to bite him in the ass of him being the one who took and held her.

Trinity was in the room yet again, unmoving as she let her mind roam, searching for the millionth time for what she had no clue about. Only, today was different. She felt an electrical shock. Something weak and small, but there none the less. She followed the smell of electricity, the feel of stimulating power volts coursing around her, as if a guiding light on a path. When she headed down the course it showed her, she heard a soft singing. A low voice which floated on the breezes, unheard by any other. Trinity focused on the soft melodic strands leading her almost hypnotically.

In the viewing room, Coyote stood. For the first time in months, the symbols illuminated.

103

Trinity found it. She wasn't as useless as a screen door on a submarine after all.

"Yes," Coyote whispered, standing and moving closer to the observation mirror. "Focus. Draw it in. Figure out where it is." He didn't talk to her over the voice distorter. He said this to himself, silently encouraging her to follow the path through its natural progression. He didn't want to do anything which might interrupt her concentration or break the direction the stone was calling her to. So he watched and waited.

Trinity continued to follow the mellifluous sound, letting it lead her. It was only as she got close to the song that other things started to become recognizable. Other sounds came through—cars honking their horns, people talking before their voices faded away as if moving out of range. She figured out it was a being that carried the soothing tune within. As she was about to grab hold of the song within her mind, it was suddenly snapped away. It felt almost as if a door had been slammed shut since she couldn't sense it any longer.

Putting her hand to her head, Trinity opened her eyes.

"Where did it take you?" The voice boomed around the room once again. "Where did you see it."

Trinity shook her head. "It wasn't clear. I was just starting to get a sense of where it was and then it was gone, like a rope was cut, the hold I had on it breaking off. I'm sorry. I did try."

"You did well. Now you know what to look for in the future."

The door opened and Axios came in to lead her back to her cell where a banquet was waiting for her, and so was Nathan.

"You must have done something good," Nathan commented. "Axios brought the food in just minutes before you got here. A reward, maybe?"

They had learned the name of the Rougarou guard a while ago from the unknown mechanical voice telling them he would be the one to return them to their cages. However, the knowledge never really mattered to her. What she did notice, besides the food, was Nathan was in *her* cage, not his. They could touch more than just fingertips through the bars.

"I guess I did." She smiled back, looking forward to spending some time with him. She was disappointed when Axios removed him from the area shortly after they had eaten.

## Chapter 10

Shara handed Zenthus the small box. He looked inside and nodded, then slipped the box in his pocket. She gave him a smile and patted his hand. She had known him for eons, but only the last couple of decades when Santanya had arrived had they become close. Shara had taken Santanya under her wing. She helped the albino woman settle into daily life at the manor. Santanya appreciated Shara's assistance. Mel had kept his word to Mani by keeping his mother safe, but Shara made sure she was not bored in her confinement.

When Shara noticed the looks between them, she knew a bit of matchmaking would be just what was needed. However, being confined to the house limited opportunities for them to go on traditional dates. Their visits were often just playing chess or discussing a book they mutually read. Occasionally, when she could, Shara would bring them dinner so they could dine and talk in private.

Shara was not sure how Mel would feel about Zenthus and Santanya together, so she helped keep their affair secret. She succeeded too, at least up until a couple of months ago. Once Zenthus was hurt when Trinity was captured, it became very obvious to anyone with eyes how close the two of them had become. With some encouragement and the realization Mel and Clarissa were happy for the two of them, their relationship blossomed even more. Now, Shara encouraged Zen to take the next step.

With a deep breath, Zen headed out to the garden. Shara had guards at the perimeters, far enough they would not be noticed but close enough should they be needed. Zen was not about to take any chances. He walked the perimeter himself, making sure all was secure. When he entered the main portion of the garden, he fixed a couple more things and then waited while standing at attention, like the soldier he was.

Zenthus didn't need to wait long; the door opened and Shara ushered Santanya into the garden. The latter stopped, her mouth agape, as she took in the transformed area. Filled with small twinkling lights everywhere, a small candlelit table stood in front of the shimmering fountain, the water sparkling from the abundant light. She took a tentative step forward, urged from the slight push on her back from Shara. Santanya was amazed at the beauty of the setting, as well as the work it must have taken for it to be arranged. Mel appeared, seemingly out of nowhere, and escorted her to the table where Zen was waiting. He pulled the chair out for her to sit and she did, giving him a glance as if to ascertain them being together was still okay. After a couple of decades of hiding their relationship, a couple of months did not change her fears so quickly. Azamel gave her a gentle smile, poured the water for them both, then left the garden, taking Shara with him back into the house. What was left was for Zen and Santanya only.

"This is amazing. I've never known the garden to be so elegant."

"You deserve a special night, Anya. You have put up with a lot and, despite everything over the past years, you have stood by my side. Regardless of possible punishment, you remained there, even when I was hurt and we were found out, our secret no secret any longer. I have waited a lifetime for someone like you. I want you to know how special you are to me."

Anya reached across the table and took his hand in hers. "I never doubted it."

He kept her hand in his as he stood and moved over to her side. Kneeling down on one knee, he pulled out the box in his pocket. "Then would you do me the honor of becoming my wife?"

Santanya's free hand went to her mouth to hide her surprised expression. Tears welled in her eyes and she knew she had the blessing of Mel and his family since he was out here to hold her chair and pour their water. Her head was bobbing up and down, sure she had no voice just yet. Zen watched her closely. He knew so little about women, but he was pretty sure those were tears of joy. As he rose from his knelt position she said, "Yes. Yes. Of course, yes." Zen gathered her in his arms and held her tight, then remained stock still when he heard her next words.

"No. I mean, no."

Zen pulled back and looked down at her. Hurt and disappointment clearly etched on his face.

"No. I mean, yes, I will marry you; just not now. Not with Trinity still missing. I don't want a celebration when so much sadness is around."

Zen squeezed her to him again. "I understand. I can wait as long as I have your promise. After we get Trinity back, then we will plan our future together."

He helped her put the ring on, indicating she was promised to him. He then moved back to sit opposite from her. Lifting the cloches, he displayed all the food choices he had prepared. All of her favorites were there and he smiled at seeing her face light up. Serving them both, they quietly sat and discussed their wedding plans for when the time came and Trinity was home where she belonged once more.

Logan entered the house, his arms laden with two paper bags filled with groceries. Ty had taken Jaz out for a while and he was thrilled to be able to plan a very special evening with her. She finally agreed to an official first date after months of asking her for one. Since he moved in with Ty and Jasmine, she felt it prudent to not let their relationship progress too quickly. Although he wondered how seeing her often over the last decade qualified as being too quick, he knew living together and seeing each other daily was an entirely different category. After all, he had to adjust to living in the human world before anything else and she had to adjust to him being around.

Tyler was a great support and had, in the interim, become a good friend. Logan could see why Jaz trusted him so much. He really helped Logan get familiar with living someplace that wasn't with his parents. It took a bit of getting used to the sounds and activity of the human world, but Tyler was great in helping him to adjust.

Now, Logan was getting ready for his first official date with Jasmine. After all the time they had spent together, they held off on anything official until now. He set the table with the candles and flowers he had bought before he headed into the kitchen to make a crawfish bisque, a citrus salmon filet with a raspberry salsa, and chocolate hazelnut truffle tarts for dessert. While everything was cooking, he dashed into the shower and got dressed. He chose to wear a button-down blue shirt and black pants. He was keenly aware of the outfit bringing out the unusualness of his eyes as much as he was of Jasmine adoring their color.

Logan just finished preparing everything when he heard Ty and Jaz at the door. Tyler let Jaz come in first, then gave the thumbs up to Logan as he closed the door, leaving the two of them alone.

Jasmine knew they were going to have their first date tonight but she had assumed they would be going out, not staying in. Logan noticed her slight look of surprise on top of the disbelief.

"I thought if we stayed in, you might be more comfortable knowing you were secured from being discovered by whoever or whatever is hunting you. And before you ask, yes, I made everything.

Tyler introduced me to a couple of local chefs at Commader's Palace and they took the time to teach me to make this meal so I could do something special for you."

Jasmine continued to look at everything. The flowers, the table setting, the food prepped on the kitchen counter. "This is amazing. You are amazing. And you look very handsome. I didn't even have time to change or get ready."

"You don't need to. You are already perfect, just as you are." Logan went to her side and took her hand, kissing her knuckles in a gallant manner. He proceeded to help her off with her coat, hanging it on the rack by the door. Leading her to the table with her arm in his, he pulled the chair out for her, waiting for her to sit.

"Such refined civilities." She grinned as he pushed her chair in.

"My father taught us to respect women and treat them well. My mother made sure I learned the proper etiquette. It's like second nature to me now. I know no other way."

"If I ever meet your mother, I will have to be sure to thank her for raising such a wonderful man."

Logan smiled. "She will like you. My mother, I mean."

Jasmine frowned slightly, although she highly doubted it, she kept her mouth shut with what she really wanted to say. "I can only hope so."

"Why would you think otherwise? I truly believe my mother would be happy with anyone who makes me happy, and you do so quite easily."

"Because of my blood, Logan. I carry within my body something many will stalk me for. If you are associated with me, they will pursue you too. Or use you to get to me, if they know what you mean to me. I am putting you in danger."

"A danger I willingly accept." Logan reached over and took her hand. "If I have to give my life just to see you out of harm's way, then that is what I would do without hesitation. I've come to care for you even more than I did when I arrived here. Living with you, seeing you every day and the kind heart you have, your gentle spirit, I could do no less. I will safe-guard you the best I can, or I will die trying."

Jasmine shook her head. "A first date is not the time to be talking of dying. Let's try to find a cheerier subject. Tell me about this wonderful smelling meal."

Logan beamed as he described the menu he made for her. Putting on some Vivaldi and lighting the candles, he began their romantic evening.

## Chapter 11

Present Day:

'*Another day,*' Clarissa thought. It had been over five years since her daughter, Trinity, had been taken without word, ransom or anything else that might indicate whether or not she was okay. Every day Clarissa searched. Every day she was out there looking for her, refusing to give up, refusing to lose hope of never seeing her beautiful daughter again. It was a mother's search of turning over every stone, tracking down every rumor, examining every clue trying to find Trinity.

It was bad enough Clarissa had to watch her whole family be killed in front of her, barely escaping herself; she was not about to lose her daughter as well.

Mel entered their bed chamber. "Oh good, you're awake. I brought you breakfast in bed." He nodded down to the covered plates on the tray he was holding as he moved towards her to set it upon the nightstand while he sat on the bed, leaning over to softly kiss her.

"Any news?" she asked anxiously, as she had almost every day since Trinity was taken.

Mel sighed and pulled back. "No. Nothing has panned out. Chip is on the lookout for her, just as he has been for the past five years. I have Zen and the others searching every corner you and I cannot go. Whoever has her, whatever their goal is, it's not even causing a scuttlebutt anymore."

Clarissa sat up, rubbing her temple. Chip was short for Chipiapoos, brother of Nanaboojoo and father to Azamel. He was also the god of the dead. If Trinity died, at any point, no matter the realm, she would have to go through Chip's territory, which passed the soul from the living to the world of the deceased. There was nothing that got by him and no way he would let his granddaughter pass. It was a small comfort to say the least, but it was an assurance she was gratified to have. Every little bit counted as far as she was concerned.

Mel took her hand in his, his thumb gently rubbing her knuckles. "I'm not sure what more can be done. After all this time, it seems almost hopeless to find her."

"Don't! Don't you dare!" Clarissa growled. The deep rumbling sound low within her chest was the sound of the wolf which resided within her, not the human she was.

Mel had spent enough time with Clarissa; her anger didn't faze him.

"I'm just trying to be practical, babe. We are looking everywhere for her. I'm having my minions scour every inch of every world imaginable. Whoever took her has kept her close to the vest. No one has seen her, heard from her, or sensed her. We are running out of options. It has been five years."

"Don't you think I know how long it's been? Don't you think I have been acutely and painfully aware of how many days have passed since I have not seen my child? I'm not giving up, though. If you are, then that's your issue not mine. She is my daughter and I will never stop until I find her."

Mel frowned as he ran a frustrated hand through his hair. "I'm not giving up. I'm just running out of options. We still don't even know which Rougarou were involved in taking her or where they brought her. We don't know what they want with her or what she has been going through since she disappeared. Whatever the fuck is going on, it's incredibly hush hush. I've never seen anything like it to where I can't get even a basis on where to start."

"I know. I know you are trying to find her. I know you are doing everything you can. I just don't understand where she is. I don't understand any of this."

"Neither do I, my love. Neither do I." He pushed the tray of plates towards her. "How about you eat and spend the day relaxing? You have not rested a full day since this all began."

Clarissa shook her head. "I don't have time to rest. Every minute I waste on resting is one minute longer Trinity is not home where she belongs."

"One minute or one hour is not going to make much of a difference at this point. You need to care for yourself as well. And in case you have forgotten, we have a son, too, who might like to see and spend a little time with his mother."

Clarissa sighed as she raised herself to sit against the headboard, leaning back. "I know I have a son. I'm very proud of him. I love him. But he has not needed a mother in years. Not since we failed finding Trinity after a year of searching. He is out in the world now. The human world and one I can no longer go."

She looked up at him, a deep sadness in her eyes. "He no longer needs his mother. He has buried something deep within himself. Logan has become withdrawn since Trinity was taken. As if he blames himself. I don't know how to reach him anymore. I don't know what to do and I am limited since he moved away. My son is twenty-nine years old and I no longer connect with him as I once did. When Trinity was taken, I lost both my children, not just my daughter."

"That's not true, Clarissa. You never told him and he is hurt you never visited him. You have been so concerned about Trinity, you have not focused on much else, including Logan. He wanted you to meet his girlfriend, see his place, take you out for dinner."

"And you know I cannot do that, no matter how much I wish to."

"But you have not told him. He doesn't understand and he thinks he is the reason you won't come see him. Baby, he thinks you blame him for Trinity being taken, for not finding her and bringing her home. He believes you don't love him anymore."

"That's not true!"

"He doesn't know it's not. You need to tell him."

Clarissa was quiet for a moment, then nodded. "I'll talk to him when I see him at the wedding. He is still coming, right?"

Mel bobbed his head in affirmation. "He is bringing the love of his life with him."

"I'll steal him away for a few minutes and tell him the truth. You're right. He deserves to know why I haven't gone to see him."

Mel leaned over and kissed Clarissa. "Rest up a bit more. It's going to be a very busy day getting the last minute preparations made before the guests start arriving tomorrow." He saw the look in her emerald eyes and took her hand in his. "Two days is not going to hurt you to rest and enjoy the celebration of another. Besides, I still have my men out there looking. If anything, and I mean *anything*, sounds promising, you and I will be right there to investigate. I swear."

Clarissa gave a gentle smile. It was a rare sight lately and Mel was grateful to see it light up her beautiful face. Her smile was what pulled his heartstrings the most. He moved the tray of food out of his way, leaning closer to her as he captured her lips. His tongue begged for entrance as his hands pulled the covers away from her.

Intimate moments between them had been few and far between since Trinity had disappeared. They were either too busy searching and apart, or too exhausted, catching minimal sleep and food before heading back out to search again. For Mel, he also had his duties as demon wrangler. It afforded them little to no time and he truly missed being with this feisty ball of fire he called his. He, too, had missed Clarissa. Needed her with a desire which could no longer be refused. He wondered if she would toss him aside, refuse him, or if she would give him what he wanted most at the moment.

Her lips parted beneath his onslaught, her tongue meeting his in a wicked dance. Her loins heated instantly as his body pressed against hers, trying to push her nightgown up and, finally refusing to wait any longer, tearing it in two from her. His hands clamped upon her breasts, teasing them firmly until her nipples scraped against his palms. Mel moved his arms behind her lower back and pulled her down under him. His silk suit glided along her soft skin and he flashed it away, wanting no barriers between them.

His mouth left hers, moving along her jaw to her neck, just below her ear, thrilling to hear her cry out breathlessly as she became excited. Her hands moved to his shoulders, her legs opened to expose her dampness. It was only then, she realized, how long she had gone without his touch and she mentally berated herself for not giving in sooner. She had forgotten how to live in her quest to find her daughter. She had put everything else to the wayside as she pursued leads, no matter how unreliable they might be. Through it all, she ignored what she shouldn't have. Her husband. Her son. Now was the time to fix both, starting with her husband.

She wrapped her legs around his waist. Mel sat up, pulling her with him. Taking her hands, he held them behind her back, forcing her to jut her breasts out to his waiting mouth. His tongue swirled around her pert nipple, tugging it, pulling it gently with his teeth, growling with satisfaction. He loved the taste of her skin, how she felt in his arms, but most of all, how her body responded to his. His demon blood burned with desire for her, his rod hard and stiff against her wet core, twitching as if searching for entrance.

His mouth moved to her ear, his tongue dragging its way along the pulse of her neck as he did so. "You ready for me, baby?" he asked breathlessly, needing to be one with her.

"Always, my love."

He needed no more encouragement than that. He rubbed his shaft over her sex a few more times before he finally lifted her slightly, settling her back onto his erection and pushing inside of her. He bounced her gently, driving himself to her very end over and over again.

He filled her, her body pulsating to his rhythm. The muscles deep within her belly tightened as her hair bounced with each thrust he made. He let her wrists go, one hand grabbing the back of her hair and twisting it around his fist to pull her head back, exposing her throat. He glided his teeth against the hollow of her throat to the life pulse of her neck. Finding the spot which beat with her heart, he suckled the skin.

She knew what he wanted, but she was also aware he wouldn't just take it. There were times she wouldn't allow him and others she did. This time she gave her consent to his silent query.

"Yes."

A simple word which entailed so many things. He growled against her skin at her permission. Somehow, knowing she would give herself over to him in every way imaginable, that she trusted him enough to agree to his greatest request and that she loved him so unconditionally, only served to make him harder. He didn't fully understand how he could be needier than before, but that was the effect she had on him. A response only she had ever elicited.

With his free hand, he held her lower back steady then sunk his teeth in against the pulse that ran against his tongue. The blood was his dietary staple. Though, before Clarissa it always came from the demons who were captured and served their sentence. Thankfully, he never needed much to satisfy his nutritional requirements and Shara had always seen to his meals. She still did as an overall. However, Clarissa was a rare delicacy he would indulge in. Her blood was sweeter than demon's and, though it did not carry the full weight of the nutrients he required, her sanguine fluid was like having an infrequent delectable dessert.

For Clarissa, once his teeth sank deep into her veins, it was an entirely different experience than any she had ever beheld. She could feel his heartbeat joined with her own, sense his emotions, feel the love he had for her and she could feel the demon he carried deep inside roar with ecstasy. It was the latter which overwhelmed her so much, she could only satiate the desire on occasion. For the most part, it was erotic and exciting. She gave into it willingly. Her eyes wide open as he drank from her while he pumped his manhood repeatedly deep inside of her. When she came, it was in a blind explosion of stars and streaks of color, a rush unlike any other. She shivered, convulsing at his touch. When Destruction started to rise within Mel, he withdrew his fangs and licked the wound closed. Clarissa collapsed in his arms and he let her have a moments rest, laying her gently back onto the mattress before he renewed his strokes with a swift, hard, steady rhythm.

Clarissa needed a couple of minutes to fully recover and start to feel the build again within the depths of her womb. Without his drinking from her, she was solely focused on the feel of him embedded within her core, her own muscles tightening about his thick, hard shaft. Her whole body tingled, her blood raced. She was very aware of his demonic abilities to keep going over and over until she was finally sated. Her stamina was quite extensive as well, due to her female and were abilities.

Before long his steady pace caused them both to climax simultaneously. Using his elbows, he hovered over her so he could continue to kiss her. He only needed scant minutes to regroup and begin again. When he was ready, he sat up slightly, slipping out of her so he could flip her around to have her lay face down on the mattress. Wrapping his arms around her belly, he lifted her bottom up so he could drive in her again. He was going to remind his wife repeatedly why he loved and needed her, as well as make up for some lost time over the past few years.

## Chapter 12

Shara and Clarissa checked the room one final time. Everything had to be perfect. White roses had been brought in and strewn about the rooms with tons of red and white tulle and big red bows. Chairs were placed accordingly about two main rooms. Candelabras and white candles sat atop red-clothed tables, which were adorned with gold plates and sparkling crystal glasses. It looked like a storybook enchanted area, just as it should for such an auspicious day.

Zen strutted into the room and growled, "Why the fuck am I doing this again?"

Mel followed just steps behind him. "Because you love her and we always do what makes our women happy."

Zenthus growled again as Mel just laughed at him. Azamel looked at the two women in the room and grinned. "Cold feet."

Clarissa wandered over to the two of them, leaving Shara to do the rest of the final check through. Reaching up, she fixed Zen's bow tie. "Don't worry, Zen. One moment of embarrassment here in front of everyone equals a lifetime of sex and happiness with Santanya. Trust me; in the long run, it's very worth it."

"Better be. All this fuss is something I would prefer not to go through. I like being Mel's strong arm. Not in the forefront of the light, wearing a monkey suit just because she wants to do the human ceremony thing."

"Demon way is not always the best."

"It would have been fine if she hadn't seen the ritual you did with Mel," he grumbled.

"I'd apologize, but I'm not really sorry." Clarissa chuckled softly.

Clarissa looked at Mel, a questioning look on her face. Mel gave his head a quick negative shake and she responded with a stern *get it done now* look. Azamel rolled his eyes.

When did he get to be the whipped male to his female? Well, granted only in some cases, and this was one of them, but he was still surprised by it none the less. Maybe he should never have told her about his best friend and how Zenthus was orphaned because of Destruction. He didn't feel Zen needed to know all of this, but he did have something left of Boralium's, which he had been holding on to for centuries. Now was the time to make sure it was passed to Boralium's son and the truth finally be told. Clarissa pointed out to Azamel Zenthus was about to begin a new life with Santanya, to start a future with the woman he loves. It would only be fair if he understood his past before he began a new future. Mel still wasn't sure about this, but he did want Zenthus to have what was rightfully his.

"Since you have a couple of minutes, Zenthus, why don't you come to my office? There is something I wish to discuss with you." Without waiting for a response, Mel left the decorated ballroom and headed down the corridor to his office.

Zen appeared perplexed and slightly worried. Clarissa put her hand on his arm and smiled. "It's okay. He has something for you which I think you will be interested in. At least, it's something you need to have."

Somehow, those words did not make him feel much better. He looked over at Shara who was too busy finishing up the final touches before the ceremony. Nodding, he headed to Mel's office as Clarissa watched him depart. She hoped it was the right thing to do. When Mel told her about Boralium and Zenthus, she wanted him to come clean immediately. He refused, not wanting to upset Zenthus. Who wanted to find out their father tried to kill the man who raised him because Destruction killed his mother and, in self-defense, his father? Mel didn't wish to burden Zenthus with such news. The male was his chief bailiff, his top guard and, in Mel's world, about the closest thing to a confidant and son, before he met Rissa. Zen enjoyed his position. Azamel didn't wish to ruin the man's perspective on his life, but Clarissa had been in a similar circumstance years ago. She knew the importance of fully knowing one's past. Better to be forewarned than surprised when it could actually do some damage.

Zenthus knocked on Mel's office door even though it stood open as Mel waited for Zenthus to arrive.

"Come in and shut the door behind you, Zen. Care for a drink? It will help calm those wedding jitters you seem to be having." He held up the decanter with amber liquid.

"Yes. I think I could use a double right now." Zen closed the door and walked over to grab the drink. "Were you this anxious when you got married?"

Azamel thought about it for a moment then smiled. "Actually, no. I wasn't. I knew Clarissa was the one for me. She had proved herself over and over again. I also remembered what I was like without her. When I was told we couldn't be together, it was the hardest thing I had lived through, so knowing she would be mine for eternity, I knew it was the perfect thing. The right thing." Taking a sip from his own glass, he peered at Zenthus. "If she is what makes your heart flutter with the thought of her near, if she is what you think about every spare moment of every day you are not together, if she is what you need to make you feel whole, then there is no reason to be so nervous. You are two pieces of a puzzle fitting together. It means you belong together. Nothing should tear you two apart. You are making your claim on her in front of witnesses so there will never be any misunderstanding of her being yours."

Zenthus downed the drink in two gulps and placed the glass down. "You're right. She is what I want, and having an eternity to be with her is all I could ever hope for."

Azamel moved over to his desk after setting his glass back on the minibar. He scooped up a beautifully wrapped elongated package and handed it to Zenthus.

"This was your father's. I know I should have given it to you sooner, but the time just never seemed right."

Zenthus' eyebrow went up in surprise. He took the box in his hands and sat on the nearest chair with it in his lap. "How did you get it? What is it?"

Mel chuckled softly. "Open it and find out. As for how I got it, well, as you know, your father was once a very dear friend of mine. However, you should know the truth about something. About him. About us."

Zen didn't stop watching him. He couldn't recall ever seeing Mel so anxious. It concerned him about what Mel had to tell him. He wondered why it mattered now, after centuries of not saying anything before.

As if Mel read his thoughts, he answered, "I never knew how to tell you. Was never sure you really needed to know. Your father should have only been in your thoughts as a good man, one who loved you and one who would do right by you. Truth is, he was all of that. He was my best friend and helped me when no one else would or cared to."

Zen was aware of all of this, so far nothing new or revealing, so he waited.

Mel unbuttoned his suit jacket and sat behind his desk

"Rissa is an amazing woman. She sees things most never do. She believes you should know the truth of your father despite my reluctance to have you think of him in any other way but as a good man. She feels to know oneself, one should know their ancestry, to know where they come from and in some cases why. Boralium had a heart for love, but he never shared it. Not even with me. It was a time when Destruction had recently taken up residence within. I had not gotten him under control to keep him locked away. There was this village near ours. I went there to seek food, hoping I would not be recognized there for who I was or what I had become. When I got to the area, I tried to barter for food. A group of men recognized me as the cursed one and attacked. Destruction emerged forth. I couldn't stop him. I wasn't able to contain him yet. He destroyed a good number of the village; the men and, sadly, some of the innocents were caught in his wake of savageness. Among them, Zen, was your mother."

Zen's eyes darkened and he lowered his eyes to the gift on his lap. He didn't say anything. He knew there was more and he was digesting what he heard thus far.

Azamel paused for a few moments before he continued. "I didn't know anything about her. When Destruction returned and I saw what was left of the village, I was in despair. I did what I could to make up for the damage which was done. I only wanted to trade for food. Boralium, your father, learned what happened. He didn't understand I didn't intend harm to come to anyone. He didn't comprehend I couldn't control the demon yet, or that its emergence was to protect me, as the host, from being killed. Next thing I knew, I was being attacked by him. I didn't blame him. I killed a woman he was in love with yet didn't know anything about. I killed innocents and I was not only ashamed, but also despondent. I could not stop Destruction so others would not be caught in the whirlwind of his vengeance. Boralium attacked me. He wanted to end my existence, and I would willingly have given it to him, but Destruction would not accept the loss of his host and returned the assault. By the time I came to, all the damage had been done."

Mel nodded towards the box on Zen's lap. "It belonged to your father. He used it on me and was one of the last things in his possession. I've held on to it to remind me I was always going to be alone in this world with no one to trust. Until Rissa changed all that. Now you have found your woman to guide you and stand by your side. She has proven as much over the last couple of decades." He rubbed his hands on his thighs then clasped them on the desk. "I am giving you both your freedom to go and do as you please. I promised Mani his mother would be safe, but I think you will do well to protect her as any other, if not more so."

Zen was unsure what to say. There was a lot to process here. He opened the gift to see a double crossbow. Carved into the wood was his father's mark. His mark. It was a piece of his past, a part of his history, even if he had been fully unaware of it until now. So many little things slipped into place with Mel's revelation, items during the centuries which perplexed him as he rose through the ranks. He seemed to have Azamel's guidance more than any other. Little luxuries afforded to him and no one else now made more sense.

Lifting the crossbow out of the box, he examined it closely then returned it to the container and stood.

"Thank you for the truth and for this. I will discuss with Santanya on where she would like to go, if she doesn't wish to remain here. Regardless, I would like to remain your bailiff. What you do here, to protect the humans, is a righteous cause. I feel there is nothing more worthy of my attendance."

"You will have a position here as long as you want, Zenthus. As well as my protection. I just wanted you to understand and be aware you have options. Whether or not you choose to take them is your decision. That and your soon to be wife. Speaking of which, it's time to start welcoming your guests."

## Chapter 13

The attendees started to gather. Shara greeted them in the reception hall. They were then led by various ushers, Mel's guards, to the ballroom where aisles of seats were strewn purposefully about. The room was filling up but there were a couple of people they were still waiting for.

Dzhihibai Manido appeared in the waiting room, almost out of breath. It had been a long while since she had seen the male. He rarely visited, in order to keep his mother safe. Hell, he suffered to keep her safe, he was not about to blow it now. However, he was worried such a congregation of folks would put her in danger once again. It was a small affair, for the most part, but even still, there were those he just wasn't sure about.

Azamel had taken every precaution he could, including limiting the invite list. He purposefully kept his brother, Jes'Sakkid, off of it, since Jes was the one who threatened Santanya to begin with in order to get Mani to do his bidding. Jes had also once owned Mani's soul, which he used to force the demon spirit to comply with his demands. Mani's soul was later recovered by Nana and Azamel after Jes lost the epic battle of gods when he tried to overthrow Nana and assume control of the Elders Council.

Nana felt Mani paid enough of a price for his involvement in the affair, and, with his mother protected in the Nether Realm under Azamel's watch, Nana returned Mani's soul to its proper home, under the condition he couldn't sell it again. Of course, Mani agreed. He may be gullible when desperate, but he was not a stupid fool.

At first, Shara was worried she wouldn't remember what he looked like, but as soon as he entered the reception area she knew who he was. She had thought the tall demon had been handsome in his own right, though now he was sporting a scar along his left cheek and wondered how he came by it. Oh, he wouldn't be the one to make every girl turn her head the first time, but there was an underlying strength of purpose to him which attracted Shara and made her notice him the few previous instances. Not that it mattered. She was an assistant to the demon judge, invisible to most unless they needed her to fetch something. Truth was, she wasn't always his assistant. She was a demon herself and she probably would have perished if not for Azamel happening upon her. She owed Mel much, swore to be faithful to him in her service, and for eons she did just that.

She was born in the Nether Realm, as were her parents. They never considered going elsewhere. This was their home and they were content. When Mel became ruler of the world, an uprising occurred. Many of the demons had no intention of falling under guidance by this youthful god, even if he did bear a demon within. The realm became filled with unruly unrest, many lashing out on whoever they came across to show their defiance to the newly assigned demon judge. In particular, massive, winged, gargoyle-like creatures, called

Waia, rebelled against the new order. They had governed the world and certainly were not willing to share the advantages of domination to a whelp like Mel.

Unfortunately, her parents had been caught in the crossfire. They both thought a change of venue would be good for the realm. Maybe many wouldn't be so scared of stepping outside of their doors. You were either with the Waia or you became their food source, which was usually done in public to instill further fear of consequences should anyone attempt to go against them. A friend of her father had been discovered one morning. Her father and mother were up in arms about the Waia's treatment and forms of punishment. By evening, the Waia were in front of her home. Shara was still fairly young at the time—nineteen by human standards. She was only old enough to know what was going on yet young enough to hide with her parents, unsure and unable to do anything to protect them.

The Waia came in force. Fifty of their ranks surrounded her home, their claws tearing it down piece by piece. Some had burst through the doors and windows. Her mother shoved her in the closet so Shara wouldn't be found. From that vantage point, Shara saw her parents ripped to shreds by the Waia's talons, claws and fangs. They were about to find her in the closet when Azamel showed up. She couldn't hear what Mel told them, but they departed what remained of the home to surround him. Destruction emerged and, in minutes, none of the

Waia were standing. She saw Destruction as he entered the house, looking for more Waia or her parents, she was unsure. He seemed to sense her though and headed right for her in the closet. Shara ducked further back in the corner. When the closet door opened, however, it was Azamel back in his natural form: Destruction had been put away for the time being. Azamel calmed her and brought her to his home to be cared for and protected. The war with the Waia had been established with the gauntlet being thrown at her homestead. Within but a couple of months, Mel and Destruction had eradicated the Waia species, the final two of which became the guardians in the reception room, standing vigil as a reminder to not go against the demon judge. Shara remained with Mel ever since the day he found her.

Mostly she was content with her role, but there were moments, such as when she watched Santanya and Zenthus together, she wished for something more personal. If she admitted it to herself, she would acknowledge she daydreamed on very rare occasions about Mani.

The first time she saw Mani he took her breath away. He continued to do that each and every time she saw him. Now was no different. The scar gave him a rakish look, which she found intriguing.

"I'm not late, am I?"

Shara shook her head. "No. Just in time, although your mother was getting worried about you."

She nodded to the guard still there. "Malcolm, take Mani to his mother in the dressing room. She will want to see him first before she walks down the aisle."

Malcolm nodded and led Mani from the room. Shara watched the two leave, her eyes focused on the sway of Mani's hips. Sighing softly, she turned back to her clipboard. Only Logan and his girl, Jasmine, had yet to arrive. She wondered what was keeping them just as Clarissa entered the reception room.

"Any sign of Logan yet?"

"Sorry, Clarissa. None yet."

"They are about to begin soon. I was hoping to see him before the ceremony." She took a deep breath, trying to calm her own nerves. "You did a great job for the wedding. Thank you for all your help. I'm sorry I wasn't more useful in the preparations."

Shara turned to face her. "I understand. You are worried about Trinity and your focus has been on getting her back. I don't blame you and I was honored to take care of the details."

"You are always taking care of the details and I don't think Mel or I have told you enough how appreciative we both are. Thank you."

Shara was slightly taken aback. She never expected to be recognized for the work she did. She gave Mel her loyalty and stayed with him for eons because he rescued her. It was her duty. Until this moment, she had never seen it as anything else. Shara smiled, a rare visage.

"You're welcome."

"You know, Shara, you are more than just Mel's assistant. You are part of our family. I know we got off to a rocky start all those years back when I first came here to be trained, but I have come to realize long ago you are only being protective of Mel. And then you have always been there for our children. I just want you to know your dedication and devotion has not been overlooked by any means, even if Mel and I have been remiss about telling you so."

Shara became a bit flustered over the effusive compliments. She wasn't sure what to say and Clarissa was astute enough to realize she probably put the matronly woman ill at ease. Giving her space, she took a step back.

"If you can, have him seek me out the moment he arrives; I will be grateful."

"Yes, Ma'am," Shara stated, turning away to face the fossilized winged gargoyles of the Waia standing on either side of the fireplace in the room. She hoped Logan and Jasmine would hurry as she didn't want to miss the ceremony.

The simple proceedings were just about to start when Logan sidled up to his mother, wrapping an arm around her waist and kissing her cheek.

Clarissa's face lit up as she turned to pull him into a tight hug.

Keeping her voice low so as not to interrupt the others nearby, she whispered to him, "I'm so glad you made it. I was getting worried." She looked around him. "Where is this girl I have heard so much about and have yet to meet?"

"She will be along in a bit. She had something she needed to do first. Mom, be nice, okay? She is really nervous meeting you."

Clarissa frowned. "Why would I be anything but nice?"

"Well, I figured you were not happy about her since you haven't met her yet. So I was fearful you might not be pleasant."

Clarissa's eyebrows furrowed further. "Logan, I need to talk to you about that." She looked around and, not wanting to interfere with the impending ceremony, she whispered, "As soon as this is over, we will chat. Okay? I owe you some explanations."

Logan was taken aback slightly, but he nodded as he leaned over to kiss her temple. Turning, he held onto her, his arm draped over his mother's shoulder as the ceremony began.

There were only a handful of people there. Nanaboojoo bound the couple together as one. Santanya looked amazing in a red gown trimmed in white. Zen looked striking in his matching red suit with a white tie. Mani stood by his mother as witness; Azamel stood by Zenthus. Besides Clarissa, Shara and Logan, the guests included

Coyote, Archanidou, Gawaunduk, and Halinois, the latter two the god and goddess of love, respectfully. There were also about a dozen of Mel's demon hunters who were Zen's co-workers.

Logan occasionally looked around as the proceedings progressed. He was waiting anxiously for Jasmine to arrive and was also interested in what his mother wanted to tell him. Before he knew it, the ceremony was complete and the guests were breaking out into small groups, each taking their turn to congratulate the newly bound couple.

Clarissa pointed to a side door from the ballroom where she knew they could talk. As Logan and Mel headed in that direction, Clarissa stopped, gasping slightly and looking around, almost wildly. Logan followed her gaze and noticed Jasmine had just sashayed into the room, Shara by her side. Coyote looked up as well, his eyes narrowing at the figure of the young woman. Archanidou frowned, rushing to Jasmine's side and pulling her back to the reception hall. Clarissa, Mel and Logan all quickly followed. Coyote wanted to, but he knew the others were watching, so held back. He didn't want to give anything away, even though he instantly knew the unknown woman who had garnered such interest was the source of the Gem of Avarice power he had been occasionally feeling and searching for.

Instead of entering the reception room, the small group entered Mel's office. Mel felt it was more secure for this confrontation. Clarissa went right to Jasmine, feeling the power of the gem calling to her and not understanding it.

"Who? What? How? Who are you?" Clarissa asked, confusion confounding her attempt at speech.

Archanidou pulled Jasmine to her, Logan stepping by her side and wondering what the hell was going on.

Clarissa noticed how close Logan was to the young woman and she realized it was Jasmine. Her furrowed brow deepened.

Archanidou moved to stand in front of Jasmine. "Calm down, Clarissa. All can be explained."

"Explained? I don't even know where anyone should begin!" Clarissa retorted. "I am the guardian. I should have known it, or some of it, existed. Even in this form."

"You were dead. The stone was destroyed. My daughters and sons removed all vestiges of the stone and scattered the minuscule remnants onto various lands. Nothing tangible exists. Except one. My daughter buried it with her eggs. She was going to hide it when she could leave long enough to do so, but by then it was too late. The stone scrap fused with the egg. When Jasmine was born, it was embedded in her heart and flows through her body as her life's blood. There is no way to remove it without killing my granddaughter."

Logan's mouth gaped. "Wait. Mom was dead? What stone? What is this all about?"

Clarissa sighed and moved to stand by Jasmine, looking her over, but it was her eyes that told her everything. They were the same iridescent color as the stone itself. The pull of the stone softly called to her. Jasmine didn't move under the woman's scrutiny, but she did look back at Logan. "I warned you." It was all she said and it seemed to have a strong meaning behind it, which Clarissa didn't understand.

Clarissa turned away, facing Logan. "You have heard I was a guardian. It fell to me as my duty once my family was murdered. It always fell to the matriarch of the family. We protected a stone which was an ancient artifact. We, I mean, I could feel it calling when it was in trouble of being discovered." She stopped. Something was tickling the back of her mind, but she couldn't quite place it. Something about Jasmine and the stone. Why had she not felt it before now? Yes, the signal was weak, and it had a different resonance than previously, but it should have alerted her far sooner than now. Had something changed when she died? What should she know, but couldn't quite grasp? Maybe if she kept talking, it would come to her, clicking into place.

Logan stood there, trying to comprehend it all. He turned to Jasmine. "This was what you were afraid people would find out? By people, you meant my mother? She would sense this, this *stone* within you. What did you think she was going to do when she found it?"

Jasmine looked terrified, her head spinning as she looked between Clarissa, her grandmother, Logan and Mel, then back again. Turning to Logan she answered him.

"I wasn't entirely sure what was going to happen; but yes, I knew your mother would sense what I was. Or maybe even your sister. In a way, I think you sense it too, though you are unsure why you are drawn to me; just that you are."

"Trinity?" Clarissa slapped her forehead. "Of course. Trinity would be able to sense it, search for it, and hear its call. Technically, I am dead, so it would make sense it would go to her to protect."

"What do you mean you're dead?" Logan looked around frantically.

Archanidou placed a calming hand on Logan's shoulder. "In a time before you were born, your mother protected a stone called the Gem of Avarice. Several searched for it, for its power was foretold to be immense. A war between the gods broke out in hopes of weakening the guardian in order to obtain it for whomever could secure it from her. They were led by your Uncle Jes. In the process, Jes killed your mother's mortal form. When she was about to cross the arch into the underworld, your grandfather, Chipiapoos, held her back, as I had asked him to. Nana, Chia and I realized this was not the full destiny of the guardian and she should not be punished for protecting the world. With the destruction of the stone, her duties were no longer required. However, we knew of her love for Azamel and his love for her. They were stronger together than separate and we felt they belonged together. Since she didn't cross the arch, we were able to bring her back to him. The rest is mostly history as you know it. With one additional stipulation." Spiderwoman nodded to Clarissa to fill in the last bit.

"Because I died in my earthly form, I cannot go to the Human Realm. It is the only one I am forbidden to go, but, my darling son, it is why I could not visit you or see your new home or tell you how proud I am of you, since you had left. I was going to tell you today, just not quite in this way. I didn't want you to feel I wasn't going to see you because I didn't love you. It's the farthest thing from the truth there could be. It was a choice I had to make and, to be with Mel, I would do it again willingly, without a second thought."

Logan waved his hands in a 'wait a minute' gesture as he tried to grasp everything he was being told. Jasmine had been hiding from his mother, and maybe his sister, because of what had grown inside her and became the source of her life's blood. His mother had been murdered by his uncle, which explained why he so very rarely saw him and why she never ventured to the human world with them or visited him for all those years. It wasn't because she blamed Logan for not finding Trinity, but because she was physically unable to.

And then it clicked for Clarissa. That little bit of knowledge which remained on the tip of her tongue finally made itself known. She paled and looked at Mel. "That's why they took Trinity, isn't it? It's the only thing which makes sense. Somehow, somewhere, they sense what Jasmine carries and they need Trinity to search it out. It's why she is still alive and why we can't find her."

Mel wrapped his arms around Clarissa. "It's a very viable theory and a strong possibility. Especially since we were unaware of this turn of events."

"How?" Clarissa turned enough within Mel's arms to look at Jasmine. "How were you able to stay off the radar from me?"

Archanidou stepped forward. "That is partially my doing. Her mother's eggs were laid in the Faefardom Realm. There is a natural protection there which hid the power of the stone, so when Jasmine was there, she was invisible to all who searched for any vibrations of the gem."

Jasmine stepped forward to Clarissa, her eyes filled with sadness and pleading for forgiveness. "I knew I wasn't supposed to leave the realm, but I..." She looked back at her grandmother and lowered her head to complete the revelation. "I had heard so much about your garden of black roses, and so I came here to see them. It's when I met Logan for the first time."

Logan piped in. "I was only fourteen at the time. I was just trying to protect her from the demons of this realm. She kept saying she couldn't come in the house or let anyone find out about her coming here."

Jasmine moved over to Logan and placed her hand on his arm. He moved it to wrap his arm around her waist and hold her close. "I came once every couple of weeks, when I could, to visit. After a while, I came more for Logan than for the beautiful flowers which grew in your garden. Someone must have sensed me and figured they would capture me on one of my visits."

"The day Trinity was taken, Jasmine had delayed her visit. I knew this was going to happen, but told no one. Trinity had found out I was meeting Jasmine in the garden and wanted to meet her." Logan lowered his head. "I was going to tell you that I thought Trin was taken by mistake. That it might be Jaz they were after."

Mel frowned. "I found out about Logan meeting a woman in the garden and told him not to tell you about her. I seriously doubted his female friend had anything to do with Trin being taken. I should have told you, my wife. I am sorry."

"As am I, Mom. I should have listened to my gut. We might have Trin back by now, if only I had spoken up sooner."

Clarissa was furious and pulled away, pacing behind Mel's desk for a few minutes. They all waited, giving everyone a chance to digest all the information. Clarissa turned towards them.

"First, without having met Jasmine, I am not sure I would have believed there was any connection between her visits and Trinity's abduction. But, I would have probably at least pursued the idea. Second, I don't understand how she is living with Logan in the Human Realm and still was not discovered."

Jasmine stepped up to the desk, closer to Clarissa. Her hands were folded in front of her in a contrite manner. "When I left Faefardom, a friend came with me and he warded the house we live in. I keep my visits away from the house to a minimum. I never, ever wished harm to your daughter or your family in any way."

Coming around the desk, Clarissa stood in front of the young woman. Many emotions crossed her features for a moment. Anger. Displeasure. Disbelief. Sorrow. Pain. But there was also a glimmer of hope and happiness. She had watched how Logan's face had lit up when he sensed her in the room, how he stood by her as they both confessed things hidden previously. After all this time, it was good to understand and comprehend what had been going on the past couple of years. Clarissa understood sacrifice for love. She made it herself for Azamel, for seeing her own family in the afterlife, and for having a family. She could not, would not, deny that to her own son.

"I do not blame you, child." Clarissa took Jasmine's hands in her own and held them. "I'm afraid we all have had secrets we thought better of elaborating upon. We did what we thought was right at the time and hid details which are only now coming to light. I wish we knew everything sooner. I wish if we had known, Trinity might be safe and home with us now instead of still with whoever has her and is using her to search for you. I really believe it is the only thing which makes sense. She was taken, either by mistake and realized for her usefulness or on purpose to hunt for what I thought was no longer in existence. Regardless, it is not your fault. You didn't ask for this. Although I wonder, having even a small piece of the gem inside of you, what powers do you have?"

Jasmine shook her head and peered perplexed at the question. Archanidou stepped up. "I have never trained her in her powers. In order to hide her as best as I could, I dampened the abilities of the stone. She can teleport into various realms, and she has telekinesis and empathy. Those are her only powers. By dampening the stone, I have also limited her natural demi-goddess abilities in the process."

"Can it be reversed?" Clarissa asked, moving back to Mel to be again encased within his strong arms.

"I am not sure. May I ask why?"

"If the stone is stronger, it might call to the new guardian, Trinity. Then whoever has her will go after Jasmine and we can find them both, as well as who is behind this."

Logan scowled. "No. Jasmine will not be used as a guinea pig, no matter how much I want my little sister back. I won't sacrifice one on the possible hopes of saving another."

"I have to agree with Logan, Clarissa. I will not jeopardize my granddaughter. I understand your frustration and wanting to do anything to get Trinity back, but Jasmine shall not lead the way."

"Shouldn't I have a say in this?" Jaz crossed her arms, a touch of anger in her voice. She felt like they were ignoring the fact she was standing in the room with them.

"No," Spiderwoman retorted. "I know you would want to help and you would agree to it, but you would be putting your own life at risk and there is too much at stake."

"What's at stake? Other than Trinity, who has been captured and held against her will for far too long? Or the agony of her family worrying about her? If I am able to do something, it should be my choice of whether or not to do it."

"Even if I wanted to, I'm not sure I can increase the power of the stone's call. As for what is at stake: your very life for one."

"Well, it's my life and my choice. Reverse it, if you can."

"And if I can't?"

"Then at least we tried and will know for sure."

"And if I can, then what? You will be hunted constantly for even a scrap of power which flows from the stone. The only way to get it would be to remove your heart from your body. You would be running and fighting for all the rest of your days. Not even the protection of Faefardom would be able to hide you." Spiderwoman turned to Clarissa. "Don't you remember when you were sought after, just because so many knew you were the guardian? Months and months of being hunted, fighting every demonic creature who came across you? Can you contemplate having such a happenstance occur again with my granddaughter who has no training? Can you relegate her to that kind of life, if you can even call it that? Don't you remember what it was like when every creature imaginable was after you?" Archanidou rationalized with a slight pleading to her voice.

Clarissa leaned back against Mel. It was so long ago, but she would never forget the constant running and fighting. She was not able to sleep much, always wary of who was searching for the stone and her in order to acquire it. She didn't even have Mel beside her for support. Alone, it was a hard existence. She realized she couldn't condone putting someone else in that situation. Ever. It was obviously not Jasmine's choice to be born with the bit of stone embedded within her. Spiderwoman was practical enough to realize the importance of trying to keep her powers limited in order to hide the stone and protect the girl as best as she could. She couldn't fault her for trying to give Jasmine some semblance of a normal existence by dampening the call the gem emitted. Undoing the restriction to the spider girl's powers would be like throwing her to the wolves. The female was not accustomed to fighting and her powers were limited, so she wouldn't know how to utilize them appropriately. Clarissa reluctantly relented.

"Yes. I remember and I wouldn't want that kind of life for an enemy, much less an innocent. Keeping the stone dampened is best."

"Thank you, Mom." Logan walked over to kiss her cheek. "I know that wasn't an easy decision."

"No. It was not my first choice, but I was thinking with my heart, not my head. I can't put anyone in the position I was in for so long. Afraid to sleep, always on the run, fighting almost every day some creature determined to end my life in hopes of acquiring the location of the stone. A piece is within her. They would hunt her to the ends of the Earth in trying to get even that little sliver. I can't. I won't put her in such a position of having to fight for her existence every day. That's not a life. It's a minimal existence at best." Clarissa's eyes shifted over to Archanidou. "You had hard decisions you had to make as well when she was born and you realized what occurred. I commend you for making them. I just wish you had informed me so I could have been more prepared."

Spiderwoman nodded. "I should have. I see my error now. I was doing what I thought prudent in hiding her from everyone. Even the guardian. Honestly, I wasn't sure what would happen and I feared for her very life should she be discovered."

"And so you should have," the deep, resonating male voice stated from the entryway of the office. Nanaboojoo stood there, the door propped open by Coyote, whose eyes glimmered with satisfaction. He lowered them quickly, lest anyone see the scheming glee which resided behind their soulful depths.

All those in the room turned to face the two new occupants. Nana strode in and approached Jasmine, lifting her chin to turn it one way then another. She tried to get out of his grasp, but it was too firm and she was unsuccessful. Moments later, he released his grip. "Yes. I would have seen her erased had I been aware of her existence. However, she is a sentient adult. Keep the spell in place and I will consider her an innocent who needs protection. I would suggest this information does not leave this room. For her continued safe-keeping, of course."

Coyote stood back, observing the proceedings but memorizing as much as he possibly could about the girl. She was Spiderwoman's granddaughter. A sliver of the stone was embedded within her heart. In order to get it, it would have to be extracted. The girl would most likely die, but so be it. She would just be collateral damage, necessary to obtain his goal. But how? When? Would he even be able to get close enough to her to extricate the bit of gem buried within her? He needed to get something from her so Trinity could keep tabs on the woman and, when the time is right, capture her to get even the small portion of the Gem of Avarice.

Mel spoke up. "We are here for a wedding. I suggest we all return to the ballroom and concentrate on the happy couple. There is nothing we can do at this point beyond what has already been discussed." He held out his arm to Clarissa. "Shall we?"

She slipped her arm in Mel's as she watched Logan offer his to Jasmine. Nana offered his arm to Archanidou while Coyote held the door open for the three couples to pass through. Coyote was still scheming and now had the perfect plan.

## Chapter 14

The music resounded throughout the room. Bride and groom so lost in each other's eyes they barely noticed their guests in attendance. They had taken time during the meal to socialize. Had they been more alert to what was happening around them, they might have realized there was a slight tension in the air. Shara sensed it, even though it was minor at best. She also sensed a pair of dark brown eyes on her, but those only served to make her nervous in an entirely different way.

When Santanya and Zenthus completed their first spin on the dance floor, the other guests were invited. Shara watched as Logan offered his hand to Jasmine to lead her to the open floor space, slipping his arm around her narrow waist. Like Zen with his new wife, Logan could barely keep his eyes off the young woman. Shara was surprised to discover she was Archanidou's granddaughter. She was well aware this was the same young girl who had been sneaking into Clarissa's garden for the past fifteen years, yet never once did she suspect the relationship of the girl's grandmother. She couldn't help but wonder why this seemed so off-putting to Mel and Clarissa.

Still, she put it out of her mind immediately when a shadow interrupted her train of thought. She looked up to see Mani holding his hand out. "This is probably presumptuous of me, but I was hoping you would overlook my flaws and dance with me?"

A smile instantly appeared on Shara's face. "I would be honored." She slipped her hand in his before he led her to the floor. He pulled her close in his arms and held her tight as he gracefully glided around the room. She was surprised at his gentleness and his eloquence.

They danced quietly for a few moments before Mani spoke. "You look lovely this evening."

"Thank you."

"Thank you for all of your help for my mother. I don't think she could have done this without you."

"I like your mother and I am used to organizing things and getting them done."

"You didn't have to do it though."

"Since your mother has come under the protection of Azamel, I felt it my place to give her some companionship. It's hard when there are not many women to socialize with while being confined, even if the confinement is for safety."

"You are very thoughtful and generous."

Shara blushed. "Your mother is a good woman."

"I know. I would do anything for her."

"I believe you have."

Mani snorted derisively. "Yeah. That I have." He looked over at Santanya and Zen. Who would have guessed selling his soul to protect her would lead her into the arms of a man who adored her. Even more astounding was reacquiring his soul, held by Jes. He thought he would be indebted to Azamel's brother for eternity. Color him surprised when Mel called him in his office and handed him the box where his soul was contained. At first, he wasn't sure he was actually seeing it, holding it within his hands. Mel had to assure him that it was his essence. He made Mani promise to never give it away so lightly again.

Mani spun Shara out then twirled her back into the encasement of his arms. "You dance divinely," he whispered softly in her ear. Shara couldn't help the chills which ran up her spine and down her arms. She had found him to be sexy, though she was well aware he would not attract most women. He was rakish with the new scar though, despite how wicked it looked.

"Do you mind if I asked how you got this?" Her finger lightly traced over the angry-looking mark which ran the length of his cheek. He flinched back angrily then returned close to her, almost apologetically.

"I'm sorry. I didn't mean to hurt you."

"You didn't. It doesn't hurt any longer. I just forget how hideous it must make me look."

She shook her head. "No. It doesn't. Actually, I think it gives you more of a jaunty, debonair appearance. I hope you don't mind me so bold as to say, it's very appealing on you. Though I am sure you acquiring it was not something you intended."

"No. I would have preferred to miss the rapier blade as a whole, but considering I came out looking jaunty and debonair maybe I should thank the bastard." Mani spun her again just as the song ended. Pulling her back into his embrace he held her until the next song began. "In answer to your curious query, I got it while I was looking for Trinity. I heard Mel's daughter was kidnapped and followed some leads that, sadly, didn't go anywhere. But some were not too happy I was snooping around, regardless of the fact I couldn't care less about their smuggling operation. This was the lesson they thought to teach me for being so nosy. Needless to say, they regretted the decision."

She stopped mid-step, causing Mani to almost trip over her feet. He looked down at her puzzled. "You were looking for Trinity?"

"Of course. Why does this surprise you?"

Shara shook her head, confusion clearly on her face. "I am just surprised. I didn't know."

"So. The efficient Shara doesn't know everything after all. The world just might come to an end." He teased her lightly then proceeded with more aplomb. "Mel protected my mother. He kept his word and kept her safe all these years. He managed to get my soul back. I owe him everything. I couldn't stand by and not try to find his daughter."

Mani pulled her close, tighter to his body after he spun her out again. He had always been aware of Shara whenever he visited. He thought about her often, and if he was honest with himself, he would sometimes fall asleep imagining her with him. Who would have thought that he would have her in his arms, even if it was just for a dance or two? He never believed she would allow him near her, much less holding her for a dance. Yet, she didn't seem afraid of him or find him grotesque. Hell, she even called him debonair, much to his amazement.

"I know Azamel had everyone looking for clues, listening for anything which might give him an idea of who took her or her whereabouts. He determined long ago the Rougarou were just a pawn in a bigger game. He was so sure it was about him. Revenge for something he did or for who he was, but with no ransom, seemingly wiped out of existence, he has been unsure what to do. And poor Clarissa has been going out of her mind searching everywhere she could, doing whatever she was able to find her baby girl. This wedding has been the first real break she has allowed herself to have. I think she feels if she stops looking, she will be condemned for it or something."

Mani looked over to the two Shara was discussing. The couple was quietly talking about something in a corner, stopping to smile at those who passed close by, possibly enough to hear. He watched as Mel brushed a strand of hair from Clarissa's face, a tenderness to that simple touch unlike any he had seen before. He wanted that for himself. He wanted a closeness with someone whom he loved and who would love him just as much back.

His mother had found it. In Zenthus. The chief bailiff almost swallowed her whole with the massive size of his body compared to hers. She was so petite and seemingly vulnerable, but if anyone gave her a moment's notice they would realize the strength she had within. He adored Santanya, but if he admitted anything to himself, he would concede he was slightly jealous of her, of having what he wanted. He looked back down into the eyes of Shara.

She was perfect. Her skin as soft as a rose petal. He had to force himself to concentrate on her words and their discussion and not get lost in wondering what her lips tasted like. He noticed this time she was wearing glasses and he wondered about them. "Do you really need that eye apparel?" he asked, totally out of the blue.

Shara blinked a moment. They had been talking about Mel and Clarissa and his searching for Trinity when the abrupt change of topic occurred and it took several seconds to switch gears and wrap her head around what he was now talking about. "No. I just thought they made me look more professional."

He stopped her movements and reached up with both hands, gently removing them from the bridge of her cute, little, upturned nose. "You are at a wedding. You don't need to look professional here." Mani tucked them into his breast pocket then grasped her forcefully against him.

"My, you are bold tonight. I never thought of you so forceful."

"So then, you have been thinking of me."

She flustered slightly. How did he do that? Put her totally off center, her head spinning in several directions like she just drank a bottle of

Kraken Rum and was having trouble standing upright again. He chuckled against her ear with a rakish laugh, as if he knew exactly how off putting he was and enjoyed every minute of her discomfort.

"I'm sorry, but I can't help myself. This is the first opportunity I have had to get close to you. I don't want proper or business-like. I want to know you, the real you." Mani pulled back again and gazed into her eyes. The song reached its conclusion and he gave her a slight dip, holding her in that position. Leaning over her, he couldn't resist and captured her soft lips with his own. Their lips joined as he assisted her to a standing position, his hand moving up her back to the nape of her neck.

Mani pushed her away, embarrassed. "I'm sorry. I should not have done that." Without another word, he strode off the dance floor, leaving her standing in astonishment, unsure what tornado just whisked around her. One moment she was talking, the next being kissed and left standing alone on the dance floor. Coyote was then in front of her, dancing.

"Thank you for waiting for me to come out to you. Saved me the trouble of going to the table and asking," he commented lightly. Shara allowed herself to be swept up in Coyote's arms for the dance while she tried to get her mind around what just happened with Mani. She didn't know whether to be upset, angry, astonished or amused. Disappointed and hurt won out. She lifted her chin and focused on her new dance partner. Only her eyes betrayed her as they scanned the room seeking

Mani out every now and again until he eventually left. By then, she was ready to leave the party as well. Gratefully, after a couple more songs, Coyote bowed out and returned her to her table to leave her alone with her sullen feelings.

Shara backed up quietly and moved to a seat at one of the tables, watching all the other couples on the dance floor. She was still trying to decipher what occurred with Mani. She was so excited he had asked her to dance. She didn't realize how just being in his arms would send thrills of pleasure through her body. She assumed he was just being cordial by asking her to dance. Their conversation had been light, for the most part. Even slightly teasing and flirtatious. She admitted to herself, she had not expected to be kissed by him, but when he leaned over and captured her lips, she realized she was lost. It was better even than she imagined. She certainly didn't want it to end. Yet, end it did. Abruptly. Just as quickly as it had started. Then he was gone and she was bewildered. Had she done something wrong? Why had he gone so quickly? Was she so awful of a kisser that he had to get away? Was her breath that bad? She didn't know what to think. Her eyes continued to gaze about the room.

Coyote approached Logan. He tapped his shoulder as he asked permission to dance with Jasmine. With Logan's consent, Coyote ushered Jaz onto the dance floor, spinning her to the beat of the music. He entangled his hand in her hair as he dipped her, moving around the floor with an expertise few might be aware of.

"How are you enjoying the wedding?" Coyote asked as he twirled his partner.

"I was a bit concerned about coming, but I am enjoying myself. Thank you. And yourself?"

"I find them a bit obnoxious. But then, I am not the one getting married and it's a chance to get some free food and drink."

"That sounds very self-serving."

"In a way, I guess it is." He twirled her out and back in again. "I overheard a bit of your conversation with Mel and the gang. You might want to consider giving Logan and the others a chance to continue discussion without you being there. Give Logan a chance to talk to his parents and understand all that is going on. You kind of threw him for a loop, from what it appeared to me."

"Do you think so? He did seem a bit surprised about his mother and my fear about her discovering me. The meeting also enhanced the possibility Trinity was taken because of me."

"Which is why you should give him some private time for him to talk to his parents and comprehend the situation better."

"Maybe you're right. I will give it serious consideration. Thank you."

"Just trying to help. I understand how difficult it must have been to keep that secret for so long."

"It has been. I never fully understood the immensity of the problem until this evening."

"Just give them some time to let the knowledge sink in. It will be okay."

"I will. Thank you."

After two songs he returned her to Logan and bowed his appreciation of his permission.

"She is a wonderful dancer, Logan. You are a very lucky male to have so exquisite of a female at your side. Thank you, Jasmine, for your kindness in accompanying a man such as I to twirl about at such a fanciful affair."

Without waiting for any further exchange of pleasantries, Coyote turned, stuffing his hand into his pocket. He had been able to obtain several strands of her hair and the necklace she bore around her neck. These two items should suffice plenty for Trinity to focus on in order to find the little spider. Coyote's left side of his mouth lifted up in a sinister smirk as his eyes darkened with the promise of his plans being fulfilled.

Shara realized her pouting and self-examination and stood to return to her quarters. When she exited the ballroom, Mani was there waiting in the hallway. He had been leaning against the wall, his one foot crossed over the other. He became upright when he saw her emerge. She stopped as she saw him, unsure whether to continue or wait to see what he had to say. If anything.

"I'm sorry."

"For what?"

"For kissing you. For taking advantage of the moment to do what I had only dreamed about. For leaving as abruptly as I did."

Shara was quiet for a moment, absorbing all of his words and the contriteness with which he said them. "You had dreamed about kissing me?" she asked, amazed he had thought about that.

Mani became flustered. "Yes. Of holding you, and kissing you, and getting to know you better."

"Why did you leave then?"

"Because I became scared about how I felt about you. I wasn't prepared for it."

She moved up to him. Her voice was soft, almost shaky. "Do you regret kissing me?"

Mani's eyes widened and he shook his head repeatedly. "Fuck, no. I don't regret kissing you in any way. I just didn't want to come across as a chauvinist or anything. I didn't want to disrespect you."

She placed her hand on his arm. "You didn't. I appreciate your consideration, but it is misplaced. I actually am glad you kissed me."

"You are?"

She grinned. "Yes. I had been wondering what it would be like."

Cautiously, he leaned down to her. "Can I do it again?"

"Yes."

Without touching her, he gently pressed his lips against hers. When she didn't run away or back up, he reached for her and slipped his arms around her. She moved her own arms about his neck. As soon as she did, his kiss became deeper. He pushed his tongue against her lips and she willingly let him in. He was in heaven for the first time in his life. A location he never thought he would be.

Shara could feel the closeness grow between them. She had thought about him since the moment she met him years ago. She knew his visits were few and far between over the past couple of decades, but she was so excited when he came for a chance to even glimpse him from afar. This was her dream come true. Better even than her dreams, because this was actually happening. It wasn't a fantasy. It wasn't a hallucination and, if it were, she hoped she would never wake up from it.

"Get a room," Mel teased as he led Clarissa away from the ballroom.

Shara and Mani guiltily backed away from each other, Shara glancing down in embarrassment that their kiss had developed into something more.

Mel stopped by Mani long enough to give him a warning glance not to hurt Shara. Mani instantly understood the silent warning and nodded. Once Mani and Shara were alone again, Mani brushed her slightly swollen lips with his thumb. "Can I see you again?"

She nodded then did something she never thought she would do in her entire life: she became bold. "Would you like to walk me to my room?"

He held out his arm to her and she linked her arm to his to begin walking towards her accommodations. Once he saw her safely there, he nodded and began to bow out. Shara shook her head. "I was hoping you would come in and stay for a while."

"Are you sure?"

"Yes." She held the door open for him and he entered willingly. Smiling softly to herself, she closed the door behind them.

## Chapter 15

Nathan held Trinity, gently stroking her hair. It was quiet moments like these which saw her through most of the days she endured alone. Her captors allowed them one cage now, when they were together. Nathan reminded her often of her promise to keep trying to find whatever they were looking for so they wouldn't hurt him anymore. But then they would remove him from her confinement for days on end. Sometimes he would come back without physical damage, others he would be heavily bruised and bleeding. She would wash his cuts, covering them the best she could. She would lie next to him and tell him everything would be okay. She would do as they commanded, so long as they didn't kill him.

He hadn't been with her long when the door opened. Axiso pulled Trinity off the bed and towards the door. Nathan tried to reach for her as she was pulled along, but he was unsuccessful. Trinity was thrown into the meditation room, as she has long since come to know it by. She was tired. She wanted to be in the comforting arms of Nathan. After over five years, you would think they would get a clue she was not going to be able to hone in on whatever it was they wanted her to find.

However, there was a table in the room this time. Something different. With curiosity, she examined the contents. Some hair and a necklace. The unseen booming voice jarred her out of her focused inquisitiveness.

"Use them to help you focus on what you are searching for."

"But these are personal items. This is hair. I don't understand. I thought I was looking for a thing, not a person."

"You are looking for what I *tell* you to look for. Don't worry yourself about the whos and whats of what you are searching for. All will become clear when the time comes. Focus and tell me where to find my desire."

Trinity had the fight taken out of her so long ago she didn't bat an eye at the command and immediately sat cross-legged on the floor. She had the hair in one hand and the necklace in the other. Through the training the voice had given her over the years, she knew the basics of focusing: opening her mind and searching for that elusive thread which called to her. She heard it on a few other occasions over the years, but she was not prepared to have it almost attack her senses as it was doing now with the items she held. They served almost as a tuning rod, drawing the call to her as never before.

She almost dropped the necklace but had been smart enough to wrap it around her palm. The hair stuck to her now-clammy skin while beads of sweat broke out upon her brow. Images, moments in time, flashed behind her closed eyelids, most of which did not make any sense. Some, however, confounded her. Images of her brother, Logan, laughing or hammering a nail in a board. Places she had never seen or did not recognize filled her senses. Sounds and smells so foreign to her she was as confused as ever as to where she was being led.

"What do you see?"

The voice caused her to focus more intently on something recognizable, even if it wasn't familiar to her. A sign, a sense of place that she could tell him about.

"Green and white awning. Lots of tables. Music in the distance. People talking. Some getting louder as others fade. The name of New Orleans is singing in my head. By the river. She is alone."

Coyote smiled at Trinity as she said those words. In all truth, he no longer fully needed her to find the wench who held the stone in her heart. He was now aware of who it was and where it was overall, but he didn't know Jasmine's whereabouts and he couldn't afford her to be followed to see where she would be before she could be taken. He wanted, needed, to know Trinity was truthful. He needed to affirm she was broken and his to command. There might come a time very soon when she would have to choose, but with his hold on her she would choose him. Whether as the disembodied, commanding voice or as the youthful form of Nathan, that was still to be seen. Either way, though, she belonged to him.

Coyote sent the Rougarou on their way to bring Jasmine to him. Unbeknownst to Trinity, the wedding reception was still occurring. He had planted some seeds of suggestion and doubt to Jasmine so she would return home first, enabling Logan to have a few more private moments with his parents. He made sure he whispered these thoughts to her during their dances while he was also busy obtaining some strands of her hair. The dancing dips allowed him to slip her necklace from her without anyone noticing.

"You have done well, my child. A more difficult test will be coming soon. Axiso will return you to your room. Rest. For you will need to be totally refreshed for what is yet to come."

Trinity stood and replaced the items back on the table. She needed to scrape the hair from her sweaty palm to totally get it off of her and it took her a moment longer than she anticipated as it clung to her stubbornly. She was anxious to return to her cell and see Nathan. Excited almost.

She was, therefore, totally disappointed to arrive only to discover Nathan was taken away again while she had been gone. She spun on Axiso. "Where is Nathan? Where did you take him this time? You just brought him back."

The only Rougarou she knew by face and name shook his head. Without a word he closed the door after locking her in the cage. Trinity found the still quietness unnerving. She wanted Nathan there. She wanted to feel his arms around her, his hands gently combing her hair while her head rested on his lap. She wanted to hear his baritone voice with that odd little accent tell her everything was going to be okay, even though she wasn't sure she believed it any longer.

How long had she been captive, with only this building of wherever she was to see? Over the years, she only had Axiso, Nathan and the disembodied mechanical voice telling her what to do as companions. She had come to rely on those three, wondering if her family even missed her any more or if what Nathan said was true: that they probably gave up looking after the first few months and moved on with their lives without her. She rebelled against such an idea at first. For months she kept hope her parents or her brother would locate her and bring her home. She kept trying to reach out to them but never got an answer, never received any sense of hope. Nathan told her she couldn't rely on them. They only had each other, he mentioned often, and in time she began to believe him.

He was a prisoner as well. Weeks before she arrived, he told her, he had been captured. However, until she came, he was always treated ruthlessly, never sure of his usefulness to his captors, never sure if he would live to see another day. How often had he whispered to her that she was his savior? Because of her, he felt they found a purpose for him. He told her often he was alive only because of her.

"I have seen you come back from the dead. Over and over again," she once stated.

"True. I can regenerate, but my immortality comes with a painful cost and there are ways to kill me so I can't return." He tilted her chin up to meet his eyes. "You won't let that happen, will you?"

"No! Of course not," she stated emphatically. "I'll do whatever it takes to make sure they don't hurt you."

He gave her a smile and pulled her into a big hug, his scheming mind seeing her resolve for freedom being chipped away. He would give her a reason to live and a will to continue to do as she was told without a fight. He would break any resolutions she had to escape by causing her to develop feelings for Nathan, to protect him, care for him, maybe even fall in love with him. Coyote didn't care as long as his alter ego did the trick and he was able to get the desired results from the young, foolish child.

Admittedly, there was a small part of Coyote who also enjoyed this situation. He hated Mel for getting involved by training and helping to protect the guardian of the gem and preventing him from acquiring it for himself. He detested Mel and Clarissa for defeating him and each and every obstacle he sent them. Each of his schemes to get the stone: setting the neighboring wolves to attack Clarissa's family; conniving to set up Jes'Sakkid in hunting for the gem; securing Xon to search for the stone; sending demon after demon to hunt Clarissa down; making deals with the Rougarou to capture Jasmine, only to fail and capture Trinity instead; and now using Trinity all this time to hunt for the stone her mother had protected. Yes. This was the perfect revenge for them circumventing him from his goal for so long. Break Trinity to nothing more than a shell of a being who wanted only to be with him, then spurn her when the time was right and know none would ever suspect it was Coyote pulling the strings until it was far too late.

## Chapter 16

Jasmine needed some air before she entered her safe haven of a home in the French Quarter. The revelations of the evening were a bit much to take in and Coyote's insinuations didn't help. True, he didn't say anything in particular, but it was his tone which put so many doubts in her mind. She wasn't cognizant of the idea her powers had been dampened in order to help hide the natural abilities of the gem. She was still trying to comprehend everything she had learned in the past few hours, if for nothing else but to ground her sense of self.

The chicory-scented coffee and the sweet smell of the herbs and spices of the city wafted over the light breeze as she walked along the Mississippi River. The lights of the city sparkled in the swift moving water. She looked up at what few stars could be seen as a result of the city lights, but they were pretty none-the-less. Jasmine was so caught with her own thoughts she never sensed them until they appeared on either side of her. She started to scream for help, but she was gone from the spot she occupied before the first sound left her throat.

She found herself in an isolated room, a sickeningly sweet cloth being held against her nose and mouth. Blackness quickly enveloped her in its blessed stillness. As she fell unconscious, the Rougarou caught her crumbling form, lifting her with ease to the waiting gurney.

Trinity was thrust into the room. She wasn't sure who the woman was or why she was there, but the call that she had been hearing only moments before had increased in its intensity, reverberating in her mind as she moved closer to the unknown female. It was all Trinity could do to not pass out from the loudness of the shrill sound in her head.

"Focus. Call the sound to you. Have it manifest itself in your head," the voice instructed her.

Trinity closed her eyes and held out her hands. She did as she was told, no questions asked. She pleaded silently for the call to come to her. Repeatedly, she requested for the piece to answer her, to appear before her. She concentrated on producing whatever was causing the ringing in her head. She thought it was coming to her. She could feel something trying to make its way to her, but then she lost focus as another sound pierced her concentration.

Her eyes snapped open. The unknown woman was now awake and screaming as she held her head. Blood dripped down her nose and from her ears. She could hear the woman's heart beat faster and the sound surprised her. Trinity reached for the woman, though whether to help her or to silence her even she wasn't sure. Before she could touch her, the woman was gone and so was the sound within her head. Trinity collapsed.

Tyler was late for setting up his table and chairs around St. Louis Cathedral. Being that he was fairy-born, he had the ability to tell fortunes and it made him enough to help pay for the everyday needs of survival in the Human Realm. He was tugging his cart along the street when he saw one of the other tarot readers looking anxiously his way.

"Tyler!" Max called, jogging towards him. "I've been looking for you. Your roommate, Jazzy. Something's wrong. Come on. Leo can watch your stuff, man."

Tyler dropped the handle of the cart, letting Leo take care of it by stashing it near Max's table and began to sprint with Max towards the Moon Walk.

"What happened? Is she hurt?"

"Man, I don't know what the four-one-one is. All I know is Sandi found her standing by the café like she was one of those freaky mimes wearing a mask of blood. When Sandi got to her, Jaz didn't know who Sandi was. She is with her now, sitting on the amphitheater's steps. She called me over and I said I would keep a look out for you and bring you there when you showed. Dude, you're fucking late. Of all days, today you had to be fucking late?"

"Tell me about it. Thanks, man. I appreciate you keeping an eye on her. Owe you and Sandi a bottle of chianti." Tyler saw Jaz and Sandi sitting midway up on the half-circle stone steps in front of the Moon Walk. Tyler added a bit more speed in crossing the street, dodging the cars while doing so. "Jaz! Hey Sandi. Jaz? You doing okay?"

Sandi nodded her greeting back, a very worried look furrowing her brow. She didn't say anything, figuring it was best to sit back and let Tyler help Jaz. They had known each other all their lives. Like siblings, according to the way they described themselves.

Jasmine gave Tyler a puzzled yet worried look, then glanced quickly at Sandi before turning to the newly arrived male, almost as if judging the woman's expressions would aid her in being concerned if the male was friend or foe. Tyler could tell she was skittish at his familiarity so he gave her a disarming smile. Although they couldn't be seen in this realm, he fluttered his wings. The sound could not be heard but it sent a soothing, calm wave of energy, which would help settle her down and even get her to accept him.

"I feel fine," Jasmine responded. "Who are you?"

Sandi spoke up. "I got her to understand we know her, so she wouldn't freak out. She says she doesn't remember anyone, not even her own name. I told her it's Jasmine, but we call her Jaz or Jazzy. She was pretty bloody. There was blood from her ears and her nose. I cleaned her up as best I could."

Tyler nodded as he sat down by Jasmine's feet. "Thanks, Sandi. I really appreciate you taking care of her and watching over her until I got here." He rubbed Jasmine's leg a bit softly then dropped his hand. His eyes searched Jaz's face. Small, telltale shadings by her jaw showed a blood trail, but Sandi did well in getting her cleaned up. Unless one knew what to look for, it wasn't readily noticeable. "Do you remember anything? Does anything look familiar? What's the last thing you remember?"

Jasmine looked around. "I remember this city. I know I am in New Orleans and I have traveled a lot of different places, but this has always been one of my favorites."

"That's right, Jazzy. You have traveled and you said New Orleans felt different than any other place you have seen. The smells and the sounds were unlike anywhere else. It's why you like it here so much."

Jasmine gave the first hint of a smile since she found herself standing in the middle of the sidewalk, unsure of anything. "Yes. That's true."

"Do I look familiar or do you see anyone's face in your mind?"

She frowned again and shook her head. "No. I only remember landmarks, smells, places."

"What is the last thing you do specifically remember?" Tyler asked again, since she didn't answer the question the first time.

Jasmine frowned, trying to think clearly. Finally, she shrugged and shook her head. "I can't recall any one thing in particular. I hear music in my head." She hummed a few bars of a Viennese Waltz. "But outside of that, just blackness. Nothing comes through."

Tyler gave her a weak smile. "Well you remember the city, and that's a start. I bet things will fall in place little by little. I'm Tyler. We have been besties since we were kids and we share a cottage here in the quarter. Would you mind if I feel your head to see if maybe you hit it or something?"

Jasmine didn't hesitate. "That's fine." She lowered her head, her hair fanning about her as Tyler ran his fingers through it, talking to her all the while.

"We also have another roommate. He is your boyfriend, I guess you would say. You have also known him since you were, like, twelve." Tyler stepped back after his examination. "I don't feel any lumps or spots where you might have damaged your skull."

Tyler honestly wasn't sure what to do. He couldn't take her to a hospital. He wasn't sure about her physiology not standing out from a full human and he couldn't risk taking the chance of causing more problems.

"Maybe I should take you home and let you get some rest? Maybe things will look familiar or the rest will help?"

Sandi frowned. "Maybe she should go to the hospital or clinic? Just to make sure? After all, she was bleeding from her nose and ears. Maybe it's a type of aneurysm or tumor or something? Maybe she had a stroke?"

Jasmine may not have remembered much, but somehow she knew the hospital was not a place for her. "No. I don't want to go to a hospital. Other than my memory, I don't feel injured in any way."

"There doesn't seem to be any lump on her head, so I don't think taking her to a place like that will help. It's more selective in what she can recall. Places, scents, sounds, that is all very generalized. But people, faces, things which would be closely related are things she is unable to recollect. If she doesn't remember anyone in a day or two, or the condition worsens and she forgets more things, then I'll take her." Tyler turned to Jasmine. "How about it? Want to head home?"

"Maybe? Pictures and things might help bring back memories. I'm willing to try."

"Do you feel okay to walk?"

Jasmine nodded. "Yeah. I don't feel like I am physically hurt or anything. I just can't remember anyone. Not even myself."

Tyler patted her hand. "It's going to be okay. We will figure out everything. Let me grab my cart from Leo and I'll meet you ladies across the street."

Without waiting for affirmation, Tyler was down the couple of steps and dashing across the street to get his gear. He pulled out his iPhone from his jeans pocket and quickly selected Logan's number.

"Answer, god damn it!" Tyler growled into the phone as he was beyond being patient for the ringing to be answered. "Come on. Come *on!* Stupid asshole fuck. One time I need you to fucking answer."

"Hello?" Logan answered, unknowingly interrupting Tyler's tirade. Loud noises came through the phone's speaker from the background so he was almost yelling.

"Logan? Get your ass home. We got a situation."

"Jazzy? Is she okay?" Logan knew the only situation Tyler would have where he would call Logan in on would be with regards to Jasmine.

"Physically, she's fine. However, there is a little issue of her memory. She doesn't seem to have one. She can't remember me, you, or anyone."

"I'll be there in fifteen minutes. I need to notify my parents and her grandmother before I just disappear."

"Fine. See you in fifteen." Tyler closed the phone and stuck it in his back pocket just as he returned to the two women after obtaining his gear.

Sandi gave Jasmine a hug, then embraced Tyler.

"I'll stop by later and see how you all are faring."

Tyler shook his head. "I think resting tonight would be good for her. Let her regain some semblance of where and who she is. Coming by tomorrow would be better."

"Okay, Ty, but if you need anything, you just call me. Jaz, I'll see you tomorrow. I promise. Get some rest and hopefully you will feel better then."

"I will, Sandi. Thank you for all your help."

Sandi turned and headed back to Max and Leo while Tyler asked Jasmine if she might know which direction their place was. She hesitated a few minutes while Ty waited patiently, hoping she would inherently sense the correct direction. Jasmine pointed towards Bourbon Street and Tyler gave a soft chuckle.

"Seems like we are always on that street, but no. We live this way." He pointed straight ahead towards Esplanade and started walking towards the French Market. He was aware she would follow him as soon as she felt comfortable enough to do so. Considering Jasmine had already accepted her name and that they lived together without too much questioning or disbelief, he doubted it wouldn't be long before she was beside him as they walked.

When they approached the little white, trimmed in forest green, Creole cottage, Logan was already pacing on the small porch. As soon as he saw them he jumped over the couple of steps to race towards them, pulling Jazzy into his embrace. She pushed him away, stepping back out of his reach.

He was flustered and hurt for a moment, before he realized she in fact did not remember who he was.

"Sorry," he said contritely. "Come on. Let's get you inside where it is safer while we try and figure everything out."

He turned and headed towards the door, holding it open for them both.

Tyler climbed up the stairs carrying his gear. "Give her time, Logan. She just needs time and everything will be right as rain."

Logan hoped so, but he didn't say anything, his eyes solely on Jasmine as she entered the abode. She looked around, hoping for anything which would generate a memory. A spark. A glimmer of something which would cause her to recall a life she didn't seem to be able to at the moment.

Tyler brought his things to his room, grabbed a beer from the kitchen, and sat in the corner of the living room, keeping a wary eye on Jasmine and her reactions to everything.

Logan stopped by the liquor table and asked if anyone needed anything. Tyler lifted his beer in a salute to acknowledge he was already good as Jasmine shook her head. She felt so out of place, her eyes wandering around to everything the room had to offer. There were some pictures of her and Logan in an embrace and of the three of them at a table with several drinks in front of them. Jaz moved to pick up one picture frame, then another. She looked in the mirror to compare her face to the one in the pictures and realized she did know both men, even if she couldn't recall them.

Logan poured a shot glass with whiskey and downed it in one shot before he refilled the glass again and moved over to the sofa. He was close to Jasmine, but far enough away to grant her some space.

"Does anything look familiar?" Logan asked. He was amazed she was accepting all of this so calmly, almost rationally. If Jaz were anyone else, he was sure they would be freaking out.

She shook her head. "I get a sense of the city and the national landmarks. I know I have been here, as well as traveled to various other cities. But, no, nothing else is familiar. Not even these pictures. It's like I am looking at someone else entirely."

"When is the last time you saw her, Logan?" Tyler asked between swigs of his beer, deciding it wasn't strong enough for what he wanted, but he needed to be lucid enough to help Jasmine. So much for protecting her as well as keeping her calm. Epic fail on the first part.

"She left the wedding about three hours ago. Said she wanted to give me an opportunity to visit with my family. She realized it had been a while since I spent any time with them, especially my mother. We are still dealing with the issue of Trinity being gone for as long as she has."

"Who is Trinity?" Jaz set the pictures down and moved to sit in the chair by the couch.

"She is my sister who was kidnapped over five years ago. We have never found her, nor has there been any ransom request for her."

"I'm sorry." Jasmine felt bad, yet something tickled her mind, even though she couldn't quite figure it out. It wasn't a face or a spark of anything she could actually remember, just a sense of familiarity, but not knowing exactly why.

Tyler spoke up from his corner. "Sandi found her about an hour ago, so that leaves approximately two hours unaccounted for."

"She didn't say she was going anywhere in particular. Just that she was headed home when she left me."

"Still. A lot can happen in two hours."

"Hey. Did I like, turn invisible or something? Stop talking about me as if I wasn't right here in the same room."

Tyler chuckled. "Well, she hasn't lost her sense of dignity or her spirit."

"Sorry. We are just trying to figure out everything from what we know. Didn't mean to not include you. Would you like to add anything? Maybe where you went after you left me at the wedding?"

"No. I don't remember anything, especially a wedding. However, I do notice, neither I nor you are dressed appropriately for a wedding. Maybe I came home to change?"

Tyler and Logan looked at each other and frowned.

"What? Do I always wear jeans to such a special event?"

Logan shook his head. "No. You were wearing a dress, but you didn't or wouldn't have needed to come back here to change."

Jasmine looked perplexed and was about to ask why when she was interrupted by a knock on the door. Logan finished off his second shot of whiskey before he stood to admit their newly arrived visitor. He was pretty sure it was Spiderwoman, since they rarely got any other guests to their abode. Mostly, because it was warded in order to protect Jasmine from being discovered.

After checking through the peep-hole, Logan opened the door and let Archanidou inside. Jasmine's grandmother sauntered in and headed directly for Jasmine, taking her face between her hands. Jasmine jerked her head away and scowled. "Excuse me? Who are you?"

Spiderwoman shook her head. "Sorry, my child. I was just anxious to see what caused this turn of events. I'm your nunohum."

Jasmine looked her over from head to toe and back again with major skepticism. "You don't look like you are old enough to be anyone's grandmother."

Spiderwoman smiled. So she remembered enough to understand the Native American word. "Why thank you, my child. It's nice to hear after all, that no matter how many eons I have lived, I still look young." Being a goddess, she could also see Tyler's flapping wings and knew he was fanning a calmness around Jasmine. She also noticed Jasmine's protection necklace was missing.

"Eons?"

"I am a goddess. So yes, eons would be a correct estimate of my age without an exact number."

Jasmine scoffed. "Okay. Now that you've all had your fun at my expense, who are you? What is going on?"

"She is telling you the truth, Jazzy," Logan said softly. "You are the granddaughter of

Archanidou, also known as Spiderwoman: a Native American goddess who protects the world of dreams."

"So, you are saying I'm like Spider-Girl?" She chuckled. How nice, they were in the mood to tease the woman with amnesia. "I suppose I can shoot webs from my wrists, climb on the sides of buildings and swing from the tops of tall skyscrapers."

Tyler snorted. "That would be so cool, but no. You can't do anything like that. You are not from the Marvel Universe of super-heroes."

Archanidou shook her head. "It's all true, dear. Oh, not that you can leap buildings in a single bound, but that you are my granddaughter and I am a goddess."

"Wrong super-hero," Tyler spat, then shut his mouth at the scolding look Archanidou sent his way.

Logan reached for Jasmine's hand. He needed to feel her soft skin, even if she didn't remember him. "Please let Archanidou examine you. She might be able to discern something that is eluding the rest of us. Maybe even see a way to heal the problem."

Jasmine let him hold her hand for a moment. She didn't know why, but for some reason she did trust this man. After all, what could it hurt if the young-looking woman examined her. She pulled her hand away and nodded in agreement. "Okay, what do I have to do?"

Archanidou moved to the couch and sat down, patting the seat beside her to be joined by Jaz. "Just let me look into your eyes while you try and remember the last thing you can. I know your memories are difficult to recall at the moment, but just try. Think to what the first thing you can recall is. I'll do the rest."

Jasmine took a deep breath. She really wasn't very sure about this whole thing, but, in for a penny, in for a pound. She stared into her grandmother's brown eyes and thought about standing on the street, thinking about various other cities and places she had been, knowing she was in New Orleans even though she didn't know where she was going, where she came from or even who she was. It was all perplexing. How did one get to be in the middle of a busy city and have no recollection of how one got to that point on the street? It's not like she materialized out of thin air. Yet, she was mystified by the whole thing, bewildered as to how she came to be there with no memory of the past. She just had that single moment in time of scanning her surroundings and realizing where in the world she was.

Archanidou pulled her hands away from Jasmine's face and shook her head. "Whatever happened, you are blocking me from seeing anything further than your first memory." She turned to Logan. "Your mother might be the one to get through. She was the guardian in a line of caretakers to that which Jasmine carries within her.

She might have more success in seeing what occurred."

Logan frowned. "I don't think Mom has the power to access someone's memories like that."

"She doesn't, but I do. I can lead her in, she can follow, and together we might discover what happened."

Jasmine stood, her hands splayed in front of her. "Whoa. I'm not up for a bunch of people traipsing around my noggin trying to figure out what is going on up there. I mean, I want to know who I am and how I forgot and get all my memories back, but not at the risk of others roaming around my head."

Logan took a step towards her, wanting to gather her in his arms and help protect her, but he saw the look she threw him and stayed back. This woman was not the one who trusted him or loved him. She didn't know who he was and didn't seem to want the closeness he could offer her. A part of him was crestfallen even though he understood his Jaz was trying to overcome some major blocking issues. Admittedly, she was a lot calmer than he thought she would be, considering she just accepted all of what they told her almost at face value. Instead, he turned back to Spiderwoman.

"Will she be hurt? I mean, with you guys poking around in her head? And, how much of her memory will you be accessing?" He asked the last question with a twinge of embarrassment. He certainly didn't want his *mother* to be seeing first-hand the times they were intimate with each other, much less Jaz's grandmother, a full-blooded goddess. How embarrassing would *that* be? Just the thought made him quiver when little else did.

"No." Archanidou smiled as if understanding his concern on both fronts. "It won't hurt her or your mother. And the only thing we would be accessing are just the moments leading up to her loss of memory. Possibly the circumstances surrounding it, but beyond that?" She shook her head. "Memories of the two of you together are in a different area of her mind. They are considered long-term thoughts and would not be accessible to us."

"But if you gain admittance to whatever is blocking them, will she remember everything else?"

"It's my hope that once we bypass whatever is barricading her from recalling her own past, everything will return. Every moment of her life will be available to her once again."

Again, Jasmine waved her hands, this time adding a stomp to her foot. "Stop it! I'm standing right here and you all talk about me as if I weren't. I really detest that."

"Sorry, baby," Logan responded contritely. "This is new for all of us too."

Jaz folded her arms across her chest as they all waited for her to say something about being called baby. After a few moments of tense silence, she looked back at the woman she was informed was her grandmother. "*If* I agree to let you and his mother play around in my head, will it actually work? Will I remember myself and all of you?

186

'Cause, really, the tales you are giving me about who I am and what you all are, are a bit difficult to swallow. Yet, there is something inside me which tells me to trust him." She pointed to Logan and he puffed out his chest slightly at the knowledge that, despite everything, something inside of her believed and had faith in him. She could be remembering the love they have for each other.

"Nothing is a guarantee, my child. However, I cannot think of anything else which might be successful in regaining your memories and, therefore, your sense of self," Spiderwoman stated matter-of-factly.

Jasmine took a deep breath, slowly releasing it. "Fine. Let's get this over with."

Archanidou shook her head. "Not tonight. It's late and there was a wedding, which you were at and so are they. It's in their home, so this is not the most opportune time to spring this little circumstance on them. Clarissa will need her rest before she can attempt what we are about to do and, my child, I think you will need your rest as well." She stood and moved towards the door, looking back at the three of them in the room. "I'll be back in the morning. We can visit them after everyone has had a good night's sleep. And Jasmine, whatever you do, do not leave this house. You are protected here, safe. Whatever happened to you, whoever did this, they cannot enter here."

"I'm not sure I fully understand, but then most of what you people have told me tonight makes little sense, unless I start believing in fairies and leprechauns," Jaz retorted

Tyler burst out laughing, spitting the beer he was in the process of swallowing before Jaz made her comment. Logan shook his head at him, telling him to keep quiet. All would come forth in good time, but right now, they didn't need to burden her with the knowledge that, at least, fairies were real and one was sitting in the corner drinking beer.

Again, Archanidou sent Tyler a scathing look and he wiped the beer off his shirt, standing. "I think I will check the perimeter."

He headed for the door and opened it for Archanidou, who bid them all a good night. Tyler shut the door behind him, leaving Jasmine and Logan alone. Suddenly, she was a bit self-conscious. Unsure what to do, she looked around nervously. "Which is my room?"

Logan frowned. "We share a room. Have for the past three years. It's this way." He walked down the hall to the second door on the left, and opened it. He stood back, waiting for her to move, to join him. When she didn't, he figured she wasn't going to at all, but then with slow, stilted movements, she came down the corridor, peering hesitantly into the room. She saw more pictures of the two of them on the dresser. A mixture of his clothes and what she assumed were hers were scattered about the room. He stayed outside, watching her assimilate everything she saw. He couldn't even begin to imagine what it was like to not recognize anyone or anything. To feel like a fish out of water, unsure who or what to trust. He felt the only reason why she had accepted anything of what they told her so far were the pictures. He had not been aware of Tyler's calming abilities.

Striding into the room with purpose, he went over to a bookcase and pulled a picture down, turning to hand it to her. "This was shortly after we moved in the room together. I had lived in the house with you and Tyler for about six months before we had our first official date. Now, please understand, we had been seeing each other for about ten years prior to my coming here, but we wanted to take things slow. We both understood we had lots of time and there was the issue of my sister having been taken." Logan looked down at the picture, which was now upside down to him since she was holding it. "We had spent the day at the beach. You and I. It was the first time we really had a chance to get away. You had talked me into not grieving for my sister. A couple of hours, you said. I need to live too, you advised me. You told me not to blame myself for Trin being gone or not being able to find her. You reminded me that I needed to have fun, to enjoy life. I felt guilty. I didn't want to listen to you, so you threw that pie in my face. Tyler took the picture of that moment. It has always been a fond memory for both of us and one of your favorite pictures. You keep it on the bookcase so it's the first thing you see when you wake up in the morning and the last before you turn off the lights at night."

Jasmine listened to him as she stared at the picture. She was just pulling back a pie plate from Logan, whose face was covered in cream and berries dripping down his features. She was bent over forward laughing. Yet, despite the fact she knew it was her and him, it felt like she was looking at two strangers caught in a moment of shared joy but was nothing more than a scene which evoked no sense of her having actually done the act. She handed the picture back to him.

"I'm sorry. It doesn't ring any bells. It has no personal meaning to me."

Logan moved a stray lock of her hair away from her face. She was so beautiful. Her light brown eyes with those unusual specks of orange and yellow held a sadness he couldn't fathom the depth of, no matter how hard he tried to understand the loss of identity she must be feeling.

"It's okay. We will figure it all out."

She gazed up into his turquoise orbs. Although she was unsure of everything, she felt him to be very caring, very concerned and loyal. It was an instinct more than anything else, but at the moment, she had little else she could rely on, so her gut was it.

She reached out, touching his cheek with her hand, watching as Logan closed his eyes leaning into her gentle touch. She had a sudden brief flash of them together. Of him leaning in to kiss her while surrounded by a multitude of vines laden with black roses and a rainbow of lights rippling over his head. Just as quickly as it had come, the vision or memory or whatever it was vanished.

She swayed slightly from the reverie she just experienced. Logan quickly grabbed her elbows to steady her.

"Are you okay?" he asked with concern.

"Yes," she said weakly. "I think I just had a memory. Of black roses, an Aurora Borealis and you leaning in to kiss me." She blushed lightly, a rosy hue appearing high on her cheekbones.

Logan grinned. "That could be just about any day over the past decade and a half. You tried to visit my mother's garden at least once every couple of weeks, and more if you could get away without being discovered. However, the good news is, you remembered something. Which is awesome, because it means you will eventually remember everything. See! Everything is going to be okay. Plus, you had a vision of me. So, maybe you can trust me a little more? Know I'm not going to hurt you?"

Jaz looked up at him. "Do you, I mean, are you in love with me?" She was unsure of anything at the moment—nervous, uncertain—but seeing him lean towards her for a kiss in her wayward memory sent excitement through her body.

He flushed and looked away. She shook her head. "I'm sorry. I shouldn't have asked. I'm just trying to understand our relationship."

He turned back to her, giving her a gentle, almost apologetic, smile. "Honestly, the question surprised me, is all. I've spent every waking moment since I first met you when I was fourteen just thinking about you. Every time you visited, I'd replay those moments over and over in my head. When my sister was taken, I knew it was you they were after and there was a part of me that worried about your safety. I guess it is part of the reason I feel so guilty. I was more worried about you than I felt I was about my own sister. I feared whoever took her would find you. No matter how much time we spent together it was never enough. Yet, in all that time, all we have shared, I only rarely told you I love you. Just so you know, you never told me if you loved me either. I guess we either assumed it was a given or it just never seemed to be needed to be verbalized, like if we said it out loud too often it would change everything we had between us. I won't make that mistake again, Jaz. I'm going to tell you every day I love you, so you will never forget."

Logan could tell she was about to say something and he placed his finger gently against her lips to keep her quiet a bit longer. When she relented to his silent request, he pulled his hand back from her mouth to hold her hand in his. "Truth is, I hadn't thought it was important since there were still so many secrets between us before. I felt in the past, there was a part of you I didn't really know. I never understood why you had to sneak away to see me or why you never came into my house. I never knew who was chasing you or why. I didn't understand why my sister was taken when we believed it was you they were after. Why keep her when they realized she wasn't you? Yet, regardless of all of this, I am still in love with you and think about you every moment of every day. I was frantic when I got the call from Tyler, terrified you were physically hurt, over-wrought with worry until I saw for myself you were okay, anxious to just get to your side. So yes, if I have to put a name to what I feel for you, then yes. I'm totally, hopelessly in love with you. I can only hope you felt that way in the past about me and that one day soon you will remember loving me. But, even if you don't, know this much, Jasmine, I will do everything in my power to make you fall in love with me again."

"I wish I could tell you what I'd kept from you and why."

He stopped her. "You did, baby. Just hours ago at the wedding. Some things even you were not aware of. We learned things about your grandmother and my mother as well as why you are so desired by whoever might have taken Trinity. I believe, when we learn what happened to your past, we will also learn who did this to you and maybe, hopefully, find my sister."

## Chapter 17

Logan entered the kitchen, fully dressed in jeans and an Avenged Sevenfold t-shirt, although he didn't look like he had slept much. Tyler put a plate of eggs, sausage and toast on the table and nodded towards him, indicating the food was for Logan.

"Dude, you look like crap warmed over. Didn't sleep well? How is Jaz?"

"She is still sleeping. I gave her the bed and slept on that rock we call a couch. So yeah, didn't get much sleep. Besides, I'm worried. What if she never gets her memories back? What if she never remembers us? Or worse, what if she can't remember how she felt about me and I can't get her to fall in love with me again? I don't want to lose her."

"You won't. She will remember or she will fall in love with you again. Just, give her some time and space. Besides, you all are going to see your mom. Between her and Spidey, they are going to do everything to help her get back to her old annoying self."

Tyler placed a cup of coffee in front of Logan and patted him heartily on the back. "Buck up, bro. You ain't gonna lose her. She loves you too much. If nothing else, that much she'll remember. Eventually."

"Yeah, you might be right and I am overthinking it. She did have a flashback of us kissing in the garden when I still lived at home. So, maybe."

194

Tyler snorted. "You just ain't slept without her in your arms for a couple of years is all. Ain't used to it."

"True, there is that, and the fact the couch smells of your rank ass and beer farts."

"What a conversation to walk in on!" Jaz rubbed her eyes, stifling a yawn as she entered the kitchen. "Not sure I'm ready for a beer fart discussion just yet."

Both men looked up slightly surprised, then Tyler bust out laughing. "Better than some of the other conversations you have walked in on. You usually say 'men' with a sardonic tone to your voice then berate how all we want is to scratch our balls and dip our wicks."

"You're in a rare mood this morning," Logan grumbled at Tyler, making a sausage and egg sandwich. He turned to Jaz. "Good morning, beautiful. Did you sleep okay?"

"I did. Although I kept having strange dreams. Almost like flashes, maybe of my memories, but nothing made sense and there was no familiarity about them."

"It's okay baby, they will come in time. Your grandmother should be here shortly, then we will see my mom. They should be able to help. I hope."

"I know, Logan. I do. I am worried though. Although, I think it's more anxious nerves than anything. Are you going to come with us, Tyler?"

Tyler looked up, his mouth full. Swallowing quickly, he shook his head. "Me? I would love to

go, but I'm not really allowed in the Nether Realm."
He then turned away, quickly focusing on making a
plate of food for her, realizing he might have said
too much.

"The Nether Realm? Not allowed?" Jaz
asked confused but still wanting answers.

Logan and Tyler exchanged looks and Tyler
shrugged. "Sorry, man. Ain't used to watching what
I say."

Logan sighed and put down the sandwich he
had just made from his breakfast plate. "Your
grandmother is a goddess, as she told you yesterday.
I am not sure you fully believe it or not, but it's
true. My father is the god of demons. He makes sure
they don't interfere with the Human Realm. This
realm. Because of his duties, he lives with other
demons in what the humans might consider a type
of hell. However, his house, *my* house, is warded
heavily. It's safe"

"And your mother? Is she a goddess too?
Why can't she come here? Why do I have to go
there?"

"Yeah," Tyler spoke up. "Your mom has
never visited here. Someone would think she
doesn't like us."

"She doesn't know you, Ty. But if she did,
she probably wouldn't like you. My mother has
impeccable taste. She wouldn't appreciate your
dirty sense of humor. Or the smell of you after you
eat garlic," Logan teased lightly.

"Ha. Ha. Such a load of roach dung. You
have me laughing my fucking ass off over here.

Asshat. You're such a dick wad sometimes." Tyler mumbled the last two sentences almost to himself, but loud enough for them both to hear.

"Honestly, man. I just found out last night why she has never been here. She can't come to this realm."

Tyler and Jaz simultaneously asked why. Logan gave Jaz a sad look before turning away. She had been there when he learned of this but didn't remember. It was a strong dose of reality each time she couldn't recall something about things they shared or just discovered. His arms ached to pull her to him, hold her close. He wanted to kiss her breathless and leave her weak in the knees, but she still didn't know who he was and certainly wouldn't allow him those pleasures he had enjoyed less than twelve hours ago. Moving past the thought, he answered them as best he could. Honestly, he wasn't fully sure he understood all of it himself.

"Long story short, there was some sort of battle, and in the process my Uncle Jes killed my mom. Although she is alive in the Nether Realm and can go to various other realms, she can't return to this one because this is where she was killed. I don't get the whole thing myself, but that is the gist of it. We, Jaz and I, only found out last night. She wanted me to know it was why she hadn't visited me here or met either of you. It's not that she didn't want to, it was just she couldn't and hadn't told me why before." He turned to Jaz. "I think it was her way of letting us know she was okay with us. Or maybe it was an apology. Again, I am not really sure. I'm just glad she finally told us. Anyways, that is why we have to go to her instead of her coming to us."

"I'm not sure I like the idea of going anywhere called the Nether Realm. What if I get stuck there?"

Logan snorted softly. "You won't, baby. You used to visit my mother's garden and me often. Besides, I won't let anything more happen to you. I should have never let you leave alone last night. I should have stayed with you. Maybe if I had, none of this would be happening now. Can you ever forgive me?"

Jasmine moved over to him. "There is nothing to forgive. I have a feeling I am pretty stubborn when I want to be. If I left alone because I wanted you to have more time with your family, I doubt there would have been anything to stop me from leaving alone." She moved around the kitchen and poured herself a cup of chicory coffee, inhaling the rich, aromatic scent before cautiously taking a sip of the velvety rich beverage.

"Hah. You are so right. Always have been," Tyler readily agreed, then looked up as he sensed an approach to the door. "Your grandmother has arrived. You ready to go?"

"Mostly. Why can't you come again?"

"Because I'm not welcome there," Tyler replied as he moved to open the door for Archanidou before she ever had the chance to knock.

"Because you are human or because you are alive?" Jaz questioned as she watched him move to the door. She was surprised when she saw Archanidou moving towards the steps. She knew he said she was here, but how did he know?

Spiderwoman glided in, greeting the three of them with a "Blissful morning."

Tyler shut the door behind her and responded to Jaz's question. "I'm alive, but it's not the reason I am not welcome there. I cannot go because of a truce the realm I come from has with the Nether Realm. We stay out of each other's territory."

"So you are not human?" Jaz asked, astounded, though considering all the revelations of the past few minutes, she really shouldn't have been. Yet, somehow she felt like Alice who fell through the looking glass to a world which was topsy-turvy from what it should be.

Tyler shook his head. "No."

"What are you, then?"

Tyler looked at Archanidou, almost as if asking permission to tell her. Archanidou nodded to him and waited.

"I am Fae."

Silence.

"What is that? Like a fairy?"

"Yes."

"Where are your wings?"

"They can only be seen in my realm."

Silence.

"Can you fly?"

"Only in my realm."

"What realm are you from? What is it called?"

"Faefardom."

Silence.

"How did we meet?"

Again, Tyler looked over at Archanidou who answered for him. "You were born there. That is where my daughter, your mother, Fern, laid you."

"Laid me?"

"You are my child's child," Archanidou said patiently. "Spiders lay eggs. And it is because of the egg that you are so sought after, which is why you live in a warded house, and why you grew up in Faefardom. It was to protect you."

"Protect me from what? This is all so confusing." Jaz rubbed her forehead. "Does this have anything to do with Logan's mom?"

"Actually yes, it does. Which is why we are going to see her today. Clarissa is, or rather was, guardian to a very powerful gem. When the gem was destroyed, my children took it to various realms and places to dispose of the miniscule pieces. Fern buried hers with her eggs. Yours was the closest and your shell incorporated the energy of the shard into your very body. It is bound with your heart and the blood which flows through you. There are many who search for any piece they can find of this stone. Therefore, they search for you."

"Are they able to get it from me?"

"Only if they kill you to get your heart. Even though it's only a minor fraction of the force which

200

once existed when the gem was whole, it is enough to change the balance among anyone who possesses it. It could also be used to find other pieces. A honing device of sorts."

"Can I feel the other pieces? Do I have access to the abilities the gem bestows?"

"No. You cannot feel the other pieces, nor would you have access to the powers of the gem. I removed that from you when you were born and we realized what had happened."

"Why?"

"To protect you. If we could dampen the effects, we hoped it would prevent the call to others that a piece still existed within you and come after you to obtain it. Although I culled your abilities, I was not totally successful in preventing the call of the stone embedded within you. For those attuned to it, they can feel its resonance when you are near or if you are exposed in an unprotected area for a long period of time. Faefardom is protected. Those spells ward this house, which is why you are protected here." Archanidou turned to Logan. "We should go. Your mother will be expecting us soon. I sent word to Shara to ready her for our arrival." She turned to Tyler. "As guardian to Jasmine, I have secured you a pass to join us, if you desire."

Tyler blinked, surprised at the ability to access a forbidden realm. Quickly recovering, he nodded. "I'm ready and willing to attend."

Logan pushed his food away and moved to the door, indicating he was ready as well.

Jaz didn't move. "How are we going to get there? I mean, somehow I don't think a car will reach another realm."

Archanidou chuckled. "True. However, I am able to open a portal to various realms. An ability you also have. We need to go outside though, where the wards won't affect us. The back yard is purposely secluded for just this reason. Shall we, my child?"

Jasmine hesitated. She really was unsure if these people's elevators just didn't reach the top floor, if she was part of a scene from *One Flew Over the Cuckoo's Nest,* or if this was really happening. She took another sip from the now-cooled cup of coffee before setting it on the counter.

"Alright. Let's get this over with."

## Chapter 18

One minute they were in the backyard of their New Orleans Creole Cottage, and the next they were in some sort of receiving room with two massive, winged, gargoyle skeletons staring at them in front of a huge stone fireplace. The blazing fire cast eerie shadows about the room, where Shara waited for them.

"Greetings," Shara said, approaching Logan for a hug.

"Hi. You must be the Queen of Hearts. I'm Alice," Jaz said, sticking out her hand.

Shara raised her eyebrow, pulling back from Logan. "Um. No. Logan's mother will be down shortly. The wedding ran a bit late last night and they only got to bed a few hours ago."

"Should we come back, then?"

From the doorway, a masculine voice boomed, despite its softness, throughout the room. "No. She will be down in a few minutes. Please, make yourselves comfortable while you wait. Can I get you anything?" Azamel gazed over at Tyler warily, his eyes narrowing.

Tyler wanted to duck behind Archanidou to avoid Mel's gaze, but he knew it would be cowardly, which he wasn't. Nor was he willing to appear weak to this god. He stood his ground, lifting his chin slightly in defiance as he did so, but said nothing.

"Hi Dad," Logan stated, taking Jaz's hand and leading her across the room to him. "Jazzy, this is my dad, Mel."

Mel looked down at her, as if searching her very soul. It sent a shiver through her, down to her spine. She felt like he was judging her and she was sure she would have been a black mark on the freshly cleaned carpet if she failed whatever test he just did.

"Shara informed us you lost your memory. I wish we were all so lucky. There are a few things I would like to forget," Mel said quietly. He turned away from her and spoke to Logan. "Have you narrowed the timeline down as to when it could have occurred?"

"Yes. We figure there was a two- to three-hour window from the time she left here before a friend discovered her like this in front of the Moon Walk."

"That is not a lot of time," Mel responded.

"No, Dad. But then, how long does it take to wipe one's life away?"

Archanidou moved forward and laid a hand on Logan's shoulder. "Logan feels responsible. Makes his words seem harsher than he means them to be."

"I understand. I would feel the same if it were Rissa who couldn't remember me or our time together."

"Do you think Clarissa will be able to help me?"

"I can only try," Clarissa spoke from the doorway as she entered the room. She greeted everyone, her final salutation to Jasmine. Taking the young woman's hand, she led her to the couch in front of the fireplace. Archanidou sat on the other side of Jasmine. Logan and Tyler both started forth to be by Jaz, but Mel stopped them both. "Let the women do what they must. Do not interfere."

Shara realized she was no longer needed and quickly slipped away from the room, anxious to get back to her warm bed and the demon who waited there for her.

"I'm really not sure what to do here, Ani. I've never done anything like this before," Clarissa admitted, unsure where to begin or even how to. She was the only one who called the goddess Ani and Archanidou allowed her to take that liberty. It always amazed Mel Rissa was allowed to get away with it when everyone else would have been smoked where they stood.

"Put one arm in front of Jasmine and take my hand. The other behind her to do the same. She will be surrounded by our arms and our beings. I can lead you into her mind. You can follow the call of the gem and, between us, hopefully, we can see why she cannot remember and open the door to allow her memories to return."

Clarissa followed the goddess' instructions.

"What should I do?" Jasmine asked quietly as she sat between the two women.

"Think, Jasmine. Focus on what you remember and keep trying to remember what you can't recall. Imagine a door which you need to open to release all your memories."

*'Well, that makes absolutely no sense,'* Jaz thought. Still, she let her mind go back to the first cognizant thoughts she had.

Archanidou used her abilities and brought Clarissa into Jasmine's mind. Once there, Clarissa could sense the stone, even stronger than she could before. Clarissa stood in darkness. Bursts of a fiery orange light would shine as if from underneath a door, then just as suddenly disappear. She followed the minute eruptions of illumination, twisting and turning down the darkened corridors through Jasmine's mind. A pounding pierced the area as she moved further and farther along. It took her a few minutes to realize what she was hearing was a heartbeat. And with each thrum, the orange glow would appear. It led her to a door, which was barricaded.

"You need to find a way to open the door," the whispered voice of Spiderwoman reverberated within Clarissa's head.

Clarissa searched for a door handle, hinges, or some way to release the entranceway, but access was unobtainable as far as she could discern. The door was solid. Clarissa tried pushing, pulling, tugging, reaching over and under to try to pry it open, but nothing worked.

"What do I do?" she asked, hoping Archanidou would hear and answer her.

"Follow the stone, Clarissa. Just as you would in the world outside. You can use your abilities to break the door, your wolf strength. You can do this, if you believe in yourself and will it to you. Just remember, you need to go to it. Calling it to you will damage Jasmine physically. The thrumming you hear is her heartbeat. It is why it matches the bursts of light of the stone."

Clarissa understood. It had been a long time since she first trained with Mel in getting her powers and learning to control them. She had to learn to move past the angry chip on her shoulder, to trust in others in order to succeed, by not letting her enemies use her own personal losses against her. She called up what she had to go through for her training. Remembered the exercises she had to do. Exercises she later passed on when she trained Logan and had planned to use in order to train Trinity. Once she was ready, Clarissa waited for the light to pulse, the burst of energy from the stone. She timed it, mentally counting, until she perceived a pattern. She hunched down, focused. Ready. She would only have one chance. She knew this much, though how, she was uncertain.

When the beam glowed again, Clarissa was prepared. She had called up her wolf senses, including strength. In one swift movement, she stood, swung and kicked the door with the heel of her foot, cracking the barrier. In that momentous second, Clarissa sensed Trinity and her own heart sped in anxiousness. Her head swam with giddiness. Was it her imagination? Would the gods be that cruel?

Clarissa took a couple of steps back, her desperation overwhelming. She ran and, with both feet, kicked the barrier once again, leaving a gaping hole. Clarissa peered inside and saw Trinity trying to retrieve the essence of the Gem of Avarice, but because it was tied to Jasmine's heart and blood, it tugged throughout Jasmine's entire being. Jasmine's body shut down to protect itself; her mind had one thought—get away to someplace safe. The stone, which was a part of her very life source, felt the pull of Trinity trying to grab ahold of it and did what it could to survive.

Clarissa's focus changed. Instead of guiding Jasmine to receiving her memory, it was now about figuring out where Trinity was. She was desperate to get to her daughter. But, just as suddenly as the barricade was dismantled and Jasmine's memories came flooding back, Clarissa was washed in the tide of them, being forced out. The contact with Archanidou disengaged and she gasped for breath as Jasmine screeched, putting her hands to her head.

Logan ran towards Jasmine, his arms encasing her to help calm her the only way he could think of. Mel was beside Clarissa, holding her shaking form close against his body as he knelt beside her. Tyler moved to help Archanidou should she need his assistance, but she waved him off, silently thanking him.

It was going to take a few moments for the others to settle down before they could discuss the complexities of what Clarissa sensed and saw, as well as get any specific details from Jasmine.

Clarissa pushed Mel back slightly. Her hands tightly gripped his biceps, her knuckles white with the strain as she stared into his eyes. Her next sentence was going to be simple, but the ramifications would be ten-fold. Her voice was shaky, yet firm and determined. She needed a moment to understand what it was she had sensed, time to comprehend what she knew but couldn't immediately process. Those few minutes Mel had her in his arms, her brain settled on recognizing one of the most monumental discoveries she could grasp. She had to make Mel believe her words if nothing else, but no matter what the consequences, the revelation would propel her forward. Alone if need be.

"Coyote has Trinity."

The room felt suspended in time as silence fell like a heavy theater curtain. Everyone seemed stunned by Clarissa's words.

"How do you know?" Logan asked.

"Are you sure?" Mel queried.

"Impossible!" Logan exclaimed as his mother's words seemed partially plausible, yet he was unsure why.

"Why would he do such a thing?" Archanidou calmly questioned. She needed to bring some sense back into the room before they all went off half-cocked and started something they would all be unable to stop just because they lost any sense of having a cool head. She would be the voice of reason, just as she always had been. It was a role she was not assigned but willingly accepted and, as a result, earned a seat on Nanaboojoo's council. He could always count on her to be fair, impartial and examine every aspect with a clear, level-headedness others failed to yield.

Clarissa turned towards Archanidou. "I don't know, but I aim to find out." She turned back to Mel. "I'll go alone if I have to, but I am going and I'm not coming back until my daughter is with me."

Logan was by his mother's side in a blink of an eye. "I'm going with you. If she is there, we will find her. Nothing is going to stop us."

Archanidou wrapped her arms around Jasmine, who appeared confused and lost about everything. The only thing was, Jasmine also remembered. Everything. Whatever Clarissa and her grandmother did, worked, yet no one even bothered to check and see if it had done so. Since she had her memories, she was well aware how important Trinity was and how long she had been missing. Her own welfare needed to take a back seat. Clarissa and Logan were right. The knowledge they might have found her, after all these years, far outweighed anything and everything else. Softly, Spiderwoman asked Jasmine how she was doing.

"I remember. I can recall everything. Sneaking away here to see the garden. The fact Tyler owes me money." She gave a smile of satisfaction seeing him frown at that memory.

"You couldn't have kept that one lost?" he quipped.

Logan didn't leave his parents' side, but he asked Jasmine the next question. "Do you remember what happened when you left the wedding?"

Jasmine nodded. "I remember I decided I wanted some café au lait before heading home and went to the Café du Monde. I was walking along the levee and heard a sound, but before I could turn around, I felt this hand against my throat and a horrible smelling cloth was put over my nose and mouth. Then blackness. When I awoke, there was a young female brought into the room. I remember she was in her late teens, maybe early twenties, tops. She was touching me and I felt like my heart was about to explode. I could feel the blood rush to my head and it pounded relentlessly and I knew if I lost consciousness again I would die. I just remember thinking I had to get out of there. I had to get home and back to safety. Then, nothing. I must have flashed myself away and the tearing from her touch caused my temporary memory loss. She had your eyes, Clarissa. A beautiful green, but her hair was darker," Jasmine managed to inform the others.

"Do you know where you were? Or who took you?" Archanidou asked softly.

"I remember when the girl was brought in, she was led by a species which had the head of a wolf and the body made from a serpent and a man."

"That's a Rougarou," Mel and Clarissa said simultaneously.

Logan added, "They are the creature that took Trinity all those years ago, but we never found the specific ones who took her, nor did we find her in their region."

"Can you tell us anything about the room you were in? Sounds you might have heard, scents? Anything?" Clarissa almost pleaded with her. She was desperately seeking the proof she needed. She knew deep within her soul Coyote had Trinity, but why, how or where she had no clue about.

"I'm sorry. I remember the, what did you call it? A Rougarou? Anyways, one of them leading the female in. I remember thinking she reminded me of a prisoner: someone who was also captured and being made to do this to me. The creature stood guard against the door. He reminded me of someone who was taking orders though, not the one giving them. I didn't see anyone else."

Archanidou gazed over at Clarissa. "If there was no one else in the room, then how do you know Coyote has Trinity?"

Clarissa added with a certainty she would not back down from, "Because, Trinity carried his scent." She tapped the side of her nose. "I may not be a lot of things, but wolves have an extremely good sniffer and Trinity reeked of Coyote."

Mel nodded. "I may not trust a lot of things in this universe, but I do trust Rissa and that nose of hers. If she smelled Coyote, then there is no doubt in my mind he at least knows where she is." He looked at Tyler, then back at Archanidou and Jasmine. "You have what you came for. Her memories have returned. You can see yourselves out."

Tyler stepped up to Mel. "Sir. I would like to go with you to help." He looked over at the two women still on the couch before facing the god once again. "Logan is my friend. You helped my ward get her mind back. I would like to assist in the retrieval of your daughter."

"Can you fight?"

"Yes, Sir. I trained with the Drayman Specialty Guards."

Jaz's mouth gaped. Mel nodded. Those were the most elite guards in all of Faefardom, and most of the other realms as well. It could be compared to ninjutsu skills in the Human Realm, but more intense and dedicated. The elite of the elite were trained with the Specialty Guards and were usually only considered from noble stock. Archanidou, however, seemed unsurprised with this knowledge.

"Get prepared, then. Surprise is on our side at the moment."

"You could be starting a feud. It may lead to a war. You know how sensitive Coyote can be. He will consider this an attack," Archanidou pointed out.

Mel guffawed. "If, in fact, he has Trinity, then he committed the first aggression against me and mine. If, by some miracle, he is innocent, he will understand the search and it will be no harm, no foul. Although, considering I trust Rissa a million times more than that sneaking trickster, I doubt it will be an issue for anything other than his being, somehow, kept alive. Because when I find

213

my daughter, I will skin whoever is responsible, including him."

## Chapter 19

The group, which consisted of Clarissa, Logan, Azamel and Tyler, arrived at the reception hall for Coyote. At the moment it was empty, but Clarissa was ready to charge through the building, kicking open every door in order to find her daughter. Mel, however, was a bit more restrained. Everything in its due course. He had learned over the millennia to take his time and examine all the angles before he attacked. It was something he tried to teach Clarissa and his son, but he also understood their anxiousness to find Trinity and bring her home. The one surprise element was Tyler. Having a Drayman Guard was unexpected, to say the least, but a benefit nonetheless.

Tyler seemed to instantly transform from the almost-gawky friend Logan had known for the past couple of years to a determined, steadfast soldier. Logan had no idea he had been living with someone who was so well-crafted in their field, or that his expertise lay in guerilla warfare with ninja finesse. As part of his studies, Logan had learned of the elite Drayman Specialty Guards but never thought he would have been living with one. He was curious to see the male in action, almost as much as he was anxious in retrieving his sister. Gone was the jovial, almost immature, light-hearted man. The Tyler who stood next to him was as serious as he had never seen before and, if he admitted it, even a bit intimidating.

Mel walked over to the massive doors and swung them open. Coyote was just about to enter the room. He smiled in welcoming.

"Greetings and salutations. Whatever do I owe this unexpected pleasure?"

Clarissa was about to charge Coyote, but both Tyler and Logan held her back. Mel's eyes narrowed. "Where is she? Release her now and maybe I'll only maim you but let you live out your miserable days."

"Whom do you mean?" Coyote asked innocently. He wasn't going to give up his prize so easily.

"You know damn fucking well. I won't play games with you. Take us to Trinity now." Mel reinforced his words with a hand around Coyote's throat, his fingertips squeezing into the skin and leaving indentations upon his column. He lifted Coyote off the floor, his feet dangling.

Coyote spat in Mel's face, chopping at his arm to loosen Mel's grip. "You are in my home and you will show respect."

Clarissa couldn't stand it any longer. She pulled back from Tyler and Logan. Her snout elongated as she fell to her hands. The fur sprang from her pores as the clothes she had been wearing tore and fell from her body, which quickly became a white wolf. With a soaring leap, she dove against Coyote, pulling him from Mel's grasp as he landed beneath her wolf body. She snarled, her teeth clamping around his neck the way Mel's hand had just moments before.

216

"Can you get her scent?" Mel asked, squatting down to take over keeping him still and letting her sniff his body. She bobbed her head when she caught the fragrance and sniffed her way out the door, following the smell down the corridors, stairs and past doorways into recesses Mel never assumed existed until now. Logan and Tyler followed after her while Mel kept a hand around Coyote to drag him along.

When they arrived in the bowels of the building, Clarissa stopped and howled. Suddenly, from seemingly out of nowhere, ten Rougarou appeared, blocking their progress any further. Tyler leapt, flying feet-first and hitting one in the chest as he twirled mid-air, landing on his feet, hunched down almost in a kneeling position. Grabbing an ankle from two different Rougarou, he stood, pulling on their legs to cause them to lose their balance. The two toppled over; the second landing on the first one he kicked, who was in the process of regaining his feet, and knocked him down again. Mel kept his focus on Coyote, thrusting him against the wall as he watched the others to make sure they could handle what needed to be done.

Although Clarissa could fight as a wolf, she was better at it as a human. She moved back until she could find an opening to get past the swamp creatures and continue her search. That was her main goal. She was willing to let the men do battle while she focused on her main objective. She paced back and forth as she waited and, at one of the passes, she bit Coyote's leg for doing this to her and her family.

Logan stepped up to take on a couple of the beasts. Clarissa watched him fight for a few moments. She and Mel had taught Logan well. His moves were precise, his aim direct. He was focused even though he wasn't as expert at it as Tyler was. Tyler's style was smooth, seamless and exact. His training far outweighed any expertise she had, making Logan and her appear as pure amateurs. However, the Rougarou were also quick with the unnatural ability that dominated the preternatural species. Where Tyler had experience, Logan was a demi-god trained on how to utilize his abilities. Opening his palms wide, he created two fireballs, one in each hand, and threw them one at a time at two of the attacking creatures. As each ball of fire hit, the Rougarou became enflamed.

Tyler had managed to disable two more in the meantime, leaving only three standing. Between Logan and Tyler, there was enough of a gap for Clarissa to leap over the prone bodies and past the three who were too busy being engaged in a battle with Logan and Tyler. Tyler was certainly quick and limber, moving about with a spryness which defied a fighting style she had seen before. She was certainly glad he was on their side and not with Coyote and his army of Rougarou.

Once she was past the poor line of defense, she put her nose back to the ground, hunting out the scent. She was almost running, her four paws hitting the tiled floor with a soft thudding. Another

Rougarou had just left a room, shutting the door behind him, when he saw the white wolf charging at him. When the door was open, the strongest scent of Trinity came bursting through and Clarissa *knew* her daughter was in that room. She leapt and caught the Rougarou by the throat, her fangs sinking into his jugular.

Clarissa felt the warm, sanguine liquid burst forth as he fell backwards. She remained on top, snarling and shaking her head, until she was sure he was no longer a threat. Pulling back, she transformed into her human form. With a shaky hand, she turned the knob only to find the door locked. Using her werewolf strength, she pulled the door off the hinges and stood there a moment, the door hanging askew in her hand. Inside the room was a large cage with a bed, sink, chair and table, and a drape around the toilet. And among all of it was Trinity, staring agape at a sight she had lost all hope of ever seeing again. Her mother.

Clarissa dropped the door and quickly searched the Rougarou for keys to the cage. She had to wipe her eyes just to see as tears of happiness streamed down her face. She fumbled with the lock but managed to get it open and flung it wide. Slipping into the cage, she gathered up her daughter and both wept on each other's shoulders.

Clarissa steered her out of the caged room. When they got into the hall, Logan, Tyler and Mel were approaching, the latter pushing a bruised and bloodied Coyote. They were thrilled to see Trinity with Clarissa yet appalled to see the living situation.

Mel punched Coyote in the gut, then face once again, before grabbing the back of his collar and throwing him into the cage and slamming the door on him, essentially locking him within the prison.

Coyote clamored to the bars of the cell, grasping them in each hand. "You can't leave me in here." He ignored the blood which slowly oozed down his mouth from the split lip he received. He certainly didn't understand why he was even still alive, but it didn't mean he was willing to subjugate himself.

"We won't. Despite my better desire to leave you skinned alive for this, Archanidou begged for my promise to contain you until Nanaboojoo comes. You will be put on trial for your crimes. I have already called for them. They should be here shortly." He lowered his voice as his eyes blazed red. A demonic resonance to his words was very evident as Mel let just a glimmer of Destruction come through. "Be grateful I have learned to control my demon or you would be skinned alive. And if I find out you have touched my daughter, there will be no council in any universe to protect you from Destruction."

Clarissa peered at him, hatred exuding from every pore. "Why? Why would you do this to our child? How could you be so cold and callus? You were a guest in our home. You knew how this was destroying our family. How could you do such a thing?" She kept a tight hold around Trinity until Mel crushed them both to his body and Logan hugged all of them from behind.

"Can't breathe," Trinity cried out from the center of the hug huddle.

As they backed up to give Trinity a bit more space, she noticed Tyler, although she had no idea who he was. She turned back to her parents. "There is another captive here. We have to save him, too."

"Another? Who?" Logan asked, ready to tear the place apart. "What was he going to do, run a brothel? Get involved with the slavery trade?"

"No. I don't think so," Trinity responded softly. "His name is Nathan. We have been together almost the entire time I have been here. Sometimes he is taken away, but after a while they bring him back. I don't know where they take him, though, or what they do to him. We have to find him," she pleaded with them desperately. "Please?"

"We will, Sis. I will personally break down every door and then some in here to find him."

"Thanks, Logan. I don't think I could have made it in here as long as I have without him." Trinity's voice held such a soft, warm tone they instantly knew she cared deeply for this man.

Logan turned towards Coyote. "Don't suppose you want to just tell us where he is? Cooperate?"

Coyote spat blood at him and remained silent. Logan sighed. "I didn't think so, but I thought I would at least try."

Tyler moved up to the cage but far enough so as not to be within arm's reach of Coyote. He blinked his eyes, their normal color becoming a bit cloudy, almost like a blind person's glassy-eyed appearance. "Nathan. Where is he?" he asked, a unique resonance in his voice.

Again, Coyote just looked at him but said nothing. Tyler blinked his eyes again, letting them return to their natural state and turned to the others, his back to the cage.

"You will never find him, Logan," Tyler firmly stated.

"No! He isn't dead. He's immortal. I saw it with my own eyes," Trinity insisted, fear etching her voice.

"I never said he was dead, Ma'am. I said Logan would never find him."

"Why won't I?" Logan asked perplexed.

"Because, Coyote *is* Nathan," Tyler responded matter-of-factly.

Logan stepped up beside his friend as the rest of them stared at Tyler like he had just grown a furry tail and saw it swishing behind him.

"You're sure?" Logan asked conspiratorially.

Tyler just nodded, watching Trinity the whole time. She was far prettier than he expected. After all, she looked *nothing* like her brother, and that was definitely a good thing as far as he was concerned. Still. She was traumatized. She had been forcibly removed from her family for years, locked in a cage in a room with no company other than Coyote who appeared to her as Nathan. Why? To touch her? To get her to trust him? Yes. It was all becoming clearer now. As he stared at her, he could see it all with his second sight, which he used on Coyote to learn the truth.

"He posed as Nathan to get you to trust him. So you would feel sorry for him and help him by doing whatever you were told. It was his way to break you without touching you," Tyler explained. "He used your gentle heart so you would do his bidding without his having to beat you into submission."

Coyote hissed. "How do you know all of this?"

Trinity was aghast. "This can't be true." She began to think of all the times she shared with Nathan. The talks they had. Were they all lies? Was everything just a trick? Deception? Was she so gullible and naïve she believed whatever she was told? Or so desperate for companionship she would trust anyone? She turned to her mother. "Mom? Who is this guy? Can he be trusted?"

Logan stepped forward. "He is my friend and I have never known him to lie. It's against his code of honor. You may not like the veracity of his words, but the truth is all he will tell you. He is Fae, so he has these powers to see into another's soul or something like that. He can tell things just by gazing into your mind. It's freaky as all get-out, but I have never known it to fail or him to lie as a result."

Tyler smiled, looking a bit more like the imp street artist than the militarily-trained soldier. "I do it as a party trick for the humans sometimes. Gets me awesome tips."

Trinity looked past the others at Coyote in the cage. "Nathan?" she questioned softly.

Instead, Coyote snarled, bearing his teeth and rattling the cage bars.

Mel turned to Trinity. "I need to ask you something. Did he or Nathan ever touch you?"

Trinity blushed, but shook her head. "I never saw this one. And Nathan only held me, but was never physically intimate."

Mel looked at Tyler, who nodded his affirmation she was telling the truth. "You are lucky in that respect, Coyote. For if there was a different answer, you would be paying the price to Destruction, Nana be damned."

"As it is, he will pay the price for his audacity and crimes. Take your family home, Azamel. I will be there shortly to discuss some issues which still need to be resolved. As for Coyote, I will take it from here." Nana appeared out of nowhere, a legion of gods behind him, including Archanidou.

Mel nodded. "Let's go home." He turned to Tyler. "Please join us as well. I would like to see you compensated for your invaluable aide today."

"I want no compensation, Sir." Again, the soldier was out and the youthful imp stowed for the moment. "But I thank you for your invitation. I fear I must decline. I am sure your family should like some private time to be whole again."

"Yes. I think we would. However, I still have some matters to discuss with you. We shall plan for a meeting about them later, then."

Tyler agreed, watching as Logan and his family disappeared, returning to the Nether Realm.

## Chapter 20

Tyler arrived in the reception chamber. He wasn't sure what to do at this point, but within moments Shara entered the room.

"Please make yourself comfortable. There is a beer and other drinks over by the table. Logan will be with you in a couple of minutes."

Tyler nodded. A beer was just what he needed. Thankfully, he didn't get intoxicated from them as easily as humans did. He didn't know how demons reacted, since Logan very rarely imbibed with beer. He preferred whiskey or wine. Tyler always figured the whiskey was the man's drink and the wine was Logan being whipped by Jazzy, which he so often told him.

It had been a couple of weeks since Jaz had lost her memory then regained it, only to have the information to find Trinity. Although Logan had remained in the Nether Realm to deal with everything in the aftermath of Coyote's deception and all it entailed, Tyler had been handling Jaz's post-traumatic stress. And she was not easy to deal with before she was used by Coyote to gain access to the stone, which would have ended her life since it was attached to her beating heart and the blood flow throughout her body. Having come so close to dying was enough to stress anyone out.

Tyler had not seen nor heard from Logan since everything had come to a head with Coyote, so he was surprised when he had gotten a message inviting him to the Nether Realm. Tyler was still nervous about coming here since there was an understanding between Demonkin and Fae to not attend the realms of either. This was the second time Ty was in the Nether Realm and, if not for the fact of Logan calling for him, he would not have come. He realized it had to be fairly important for Logan to take the risk of having a Fae where one didn't belong, especially for a second time.

A part of him wondered if it were a trap and he was being lured there in order to be arrested and thrown into one of the dungeons he had heard about. A place for those who broke Mel's law. Depending on the crime, it would also decree any possible additional punishment. However, Ty was of noble birth. Should he disappear without checking in at the appropriate time, there would be a search for him. When they discovered where he was, there would be a Fae uprising, which would not bode well for any. He wasn't scared of being arrested or even tortured. He was well-trained, as any soldier would have been. However, Logan was a friend; he couldn't believe it was a trap. Still, the thought did run through his mind, even though he discounted it as irrational and ridiculous.

Yep, he needed this beer. Twisting off the cap and hearing the comforting pop and fizz of the vacuum being released from the bottle, he tilted it back against his greedy lips. He realized, even though he would *never* admit it, that it wasn't, in fact, worry about being arrested or tortured, but his desirous longing to see Trinity again. Even in those few minutes he had met her, there was a strength of character and presence which caught his attention. The fact she was also more beautiful than any Fae or human he had ever met didn't help his circumstances. If he were truthful to even himself, he had not stopped thinking about her. Yeah, there was something the Fae would appreciate. Nobility with Demonkin. Oh, he could see it now. He rolled his eyes and finished off the bottle of beer, hoping for anything which might resemble even a small buzz. Sadly, nothing.

He tossed the bottle in the trash just as Logan entered the room. Logan looked worn and weary, but he smiled as he saw Ty standing there, grateful for even this small connection-by-association to Jaz. Logan strode over and grasped Ty's hand, pulling him into a bro hug.

"Damn, it's good to see you. How have you been? How is Jazzy?"

Tyler patted his back a couple of times in the middle of the hug then backed up. "She is managing. It would be easier if you were there sleeping next to her. She keeps crying out in her sleep for you; although, the past couple of nights she has been sleeping a bit better."

"I want to see her. I am anxious to go back home, but Mom and Trin still need me here. Dad has been dealing with the Elders Council and Coyote's trial, which, as you know, can be slower than slugs racing snails or watching paint dry. I have heard Dad has almost killed him twice when he became arrogant.

"Trinity still doesn't believe he was Nathan, even after they made Coyote prove it by changing his form."

"How is Trinity doing, otherwise?"

Logan shook his head and sighed deeply. "She is suffering and I don't know what to do for her."

"Is she in pain?"

"Only mentally. She was stuck in that room—in that prison—for so fucking long, she doesn't know how to socialize anymore. And with Coyote fucking with her as Nathan, she is unsure what to believe or disbelieve. She is having a hard time and it's driving me bonkers since I can't seem help her. I don't know *how* to help her."

"You know, it's not my place to say anything, but then you know me better than that. Maybe this isn't such a good place for her."

"What do you mean?"

"Well, she was a virtual prisoner before she was taken. You have told me how you could rarely leave the house because of possible enemies of your father, so it wasn't safe. When you did leave, you were surrounded by guards. I assume it was the same with her. Then she was taken and stuck in a different, but very similar, cage before she was found again after so long, only to be returned to the first gilded cage she was originally confined in."

"It's not like we are not trying to get her out, but having her just leave her room for a meal is like pulling teeth."

"What incentive does she have to leave her room? Listen, dude, all I am saying is maybe take her out someplace more interesting. Someplace she might *want* to go or visit or see. Something which will prove to her she is still not a captured prisoner. I, um. Well, I could even go with you and help guard her if you would feel safer with her being out."

"I don't know if she will go, but that's why I called you here. The only place she ever wanted to visit, that I know of, was Faefardom. She wanted me to sneak her into the realm just to have a look around, but that was before she was taken. Who knows if she is interested in anything anymore? She sure doesn't seem like it. I was hoping I could take her there to see it. You know, get her outside and show her she is not under Coyote and the Rougarou anymore."

Tyler thought a moment. "I will make sure she gets an invitation. Give me a day. Talk it up. Get her excited to see it, and I will be your personal escort. I just need to make a few arrangements for your visit." He ran a hand through his hair. "I'll make sure you both can visit. Your parents, too. Was there anything else you needed from me?"

"Actually, yes. I was hoping you would talk to Jazzy. I need to see her. I miss her."

"Trying to make me more useless?" Tyler teased. He hadn't been fully needed to protect Jasmine since Logan came, and he knew soon he would no longer have a job. He might even be forced to return to Faefardom and take on other duties, something he was not too keen about. He enjoyed the free spirit of the human world: the parties, the tattoos, the general freedom he was allowed to have, which he wouldn't once he returned to Faefardom.

"Useless is your middle name," Logan teased him back. "Actually, no. Listen, Ty. I need your help with Trinity. I've seen you work with Jaz and know you can calm her when necessary. I figure it's one of your special abilities. I am hoping you can help Trinity the same way. If she is a little less skittish, maybe she will settle back into her life better. Maybe even begin a new and better chapter of it. Could you help? Would you be interested?"

Tyler hemmed and hawed a bit, shifting uncomfortably. If he agreed, it would mean spending more time with Trinity, and he wasn't sure he could hide his growing affection for her. He was known as not interested in anyone except to sow his oats as often as any mare would let him. Rarely the same twice; he never wanted to get attached to anyone. Until he met Trinity. Even under the direst circumstances of being held captive for so long, something about her caught his attention. He couldn't put his finger on it, but he had to admit he had done nothing but think about her since he first saw her. Out of respect for the man-code, he wasn't going to say or do anything. If Logan figured out how he was really beginning to feel, it would cause innumerable problems, to say the least.

"Even if I did agree, I couldn't be of much help. She's here and I'm already pushing my luck by breaching the contract between our realms twice already. Besides, she has been through a hell of her own. She sure as fuck don't need a screw up like me protecting her. Why ask?"

"I just thought if you could help, you might be interested in getting her back into the world of reality. I trust you, because I know she would be in good hands, like Jaz has been all these years."

"I would still guard her, if you wanted me to. You just got to bring her to the Human Realm or something."

"She still has this thing for Nathan. Fucking Coyote, screwing with her head like that. I would love to get my hands on him for five minutes without the council looking, but Dad has already tried, from what I heard. Anyways, I just thought, maybe you could help me get her out more. If I could bring her to the Human Realm and away from here for a bit, get her among others, maybe she would adapt better."

"Maybe. Or it might make things worse if she becomes too frightened."

"I thought about that, which is why I thought of your ability. What do you think?"

"I don't know her very well, Logan, but despite everything she went through, she still seemed amazingly strong when we got her. She wasn't going to leave without Nathan. She was willing to fight for him, for us to find him. Meek and frightened like some little mouse is not the impression I got. She didn't cower or back down in any way, despite being restricted, and fuck-only-knows how she was treated for as long as she had been there. You would know these subtleties better than I. Listen, bro. If you want, I will help you help her however you wish."

"You are great, Ty. Let me know if you can make those arrangements and when they are done for Faefardom. I'll call you when things are settled for her to come to the Human Realm."

"I'll get some planning done for her visit to the Human Realm. Might even give Jazzy some of the planning work, help her get her mind off of her experience and give her something to look forward to doing."

"Do you think she will be okay with Trinity?" Logan asked worriedly. "I'm afraid she will hold it against my sister for what happened."

Tyler shook his head. "No. Jaz has said the whole time, she knew it was Coyote and the Rougarou and Trinity was only a victim who was being manipulated. If there is any resentment still there, she has not indicated anything to that effect."

Logan sighed with relief. "I was worried she would hate my sister because of what happened and, in association, me."

"No, dude. She loves you too much and you know she had felt awful about the loss of your sister. There is no way she would think anything less of her or you."

"Still. I had to wonder."

"I get it. I do. I will call you when I have everything planned for tomorrow."

Logan shook his hand, his other slapping his shoulder. "Tell Jaz I've not forgotten about her and I miss her terribly."

"She knows, dude. I'll tell her, though, and suffer the eye roll I will probably get as a result." Chuckling, Ty headed back through the portal.

Taking a couple of deep breaths, Logan braced himself then headed back to help his mom with Trinity.

## Chapter 21

Tyler had to pull a lot of strings, use up favors he had collected over the years and make a few promises he would have preferred not to, in order to get the two visitor passes: one for Trinity and the other for Logan. He was going to get additional ones for Clarissa and Mel, but after talking with Logan was informed they would not be going. Clarissa wanted to, but she also realized her children didn't need their *mom* tagging along.

Although she was nervous letting either of them, especially Trinity, out of her sight for any extended period of time, she also believed it was a necessary step. Trinity needed to have a bit of her independence while Clarissa needed to overcome her motherly overprotection, which was a bit smothering. She knew she had every right to want to put her daughter in bubble wrap, but it wouldn't be very conducive to any mental and emotional healing, which needed to be accomplished by both of them. Clarissa spent years hunting and searching for her daughter. She was as emotionally raw and exhausted as her child must be.

It had seemed odd for Clarissa to awaken with no plan on where to search or who to beat up in order to get the next clue as to where her daughter was being detained. The first night they brought her home, Clarissa stayed in the same room as Trinity so every time she opened her eyes, her daughter was visible.

Years ago, Trinity might have balked at the over-concern she was being shown, but truthfully, she appreciated the security she felt with her mother being so close. She was sure it would take a while for Trinity to feel secure again. Five years being alone, except for Nathan and her guards, would take time to overcome. Trinity knew she had to adapt to many things again, some new and some old.

Trinity's mother even encouraged Logan to take her to Faefardom, just to give her opportunities away from being cooped up in her room. True, it was someplace Trinity had always wanted to visit and had even blackmailed Logan into taking her there once many moons ago. So why wasn't she excited about the prospect now?

Trinity realized part of it was because she had pictured Nathan with her once they were both free. She believed they would spend their time together, maybe even grow old together. How could she have been so wrong about him? How could she have not known he was lying to her? True, she had no experience with boys other than the guards, her father, or her brother before she was taken from her home, but she didn't think she was so stupidly naïve. Yet, the entire time Nathan wasn't real. He didn't exist. Someone she had cared for, maybe even loved, was nothing but a lie, an illusion. How was she supposed to deal with that? How was she supposed to trust anyone? Nathan told her what she wanted to hear, gave her the comfort she longed for and wormed his way into her heart. She would have done anything for him, *had* done everything she could to help keep him safe, when in truth, he was never in danger. Talk about screwing with one's head!

Trinity didn't want to go on Logan's planned field trip. She wasn't ready to leave the sanctity of her home when she barely got past the inviolability of her room. Logan and Tyler knocked on her door. When she finally answered, Logan and Tyler waited until she invited them inside. They both were trying to be respectful of her or they would have just each grabbed an arm and toted her away. Definitely not the most appropriate course of action with someone who was kidnapped and held against their will for so long.

"Hi, Sis. You remember Tyler? My buddy?"

Trinity nodded. "Yes. He was part of the, I mean, he was with you when you all came and got me."

Tyler walked over to her and held his hand out for hers. When she eventually gave it to him, he bowed low over it. "My greatest pleasure in being a participant in your freedom," he said graciously.

Trinity blushed and looked at Logan, confusion etching her features. Logan still had a difficult time adjusting to seeing his sister more mature in stature, as well as appearance, since she had been gone. It tore at his heart they could not find her sooner. If only he had told them about Jazzy sooner, or that his girlfriend was most likely what they had been seeking when they took his baby sister. But, hindsight was twenty-twenty when it came to the past, and what ifs would drive any sane person bonkers.

"Don't mind him. He is always weird, but he is harmless."

Tyler threw Logan a *'shut it, asshole'* look, which only made Logan smirk.

Trinity pulled her hand back. "Thank you for securing the passes to visit your realm, but I am not going after all."

"Of course you are going. You have no idea how difficult getting these passes for folks from the Nether Realm were to achieve. I had to use a lot of persuasion to get them and I hope you won't deny me the wonderfulness of your company. I have so much to show you, such as the Trident Falls and the Singing Springs. It's so beautiful; I know you will absolutely adore it. Our skies are a pale lavender and the clouds are sky blue. Please, don't disappoint me from showing you around. I promise you will have a great time and you will be safe. You have my word on that."

"And mine. On you being safe, I mean. I won't let anything happen to you. Faefardom has some sort of natural ability to block the call of the stone. Jaz will be with us and I so want you to get to know her better. She is so anxious to spend time with you."

"She isn't upset with me for hurting her?"

Both the men shook their heads. "No," Logan stated firmly. "She knows you were only doing what you were told to do. She realizes none of it was your fault or doing. She has been as concerned as the rest of us in just getting you home again, and she is so thrilled we have achieved such an accomplishment."

"Then where is she?"

"Actually, Jazzy is already there waiting for us and making a picnic lunch for us to enjoy. The weather is beautifully warm and sunny, which is normal for us. She is making some sandwiches and salads to bring with us for some of our sightseeing adventures," Tyler replied, taking her hand once again. "Please, say you have changed your mind and will go to my magical realm." Tyler's eyes beseeched hers. He had told Logan he would use his wings if he needed to in order to get her to be calm enough to want to go with them, but he was hoping his own enamoring, personable self would suffice.

Trinity hesitated. Tyler certainly made some charming and convincing arguments and really seemed to want her to go. However, it was Logan who seemed to be silently pleading, which altered her original resolve. "Okay," she said rather reluctantly. "I'll go, but only on the condition that when I am ready to return, I am allowed to do so."

"Of course," Tyler said.

"Sure, Sis. You say the word and we are back here. But let's give it a chance and really see it."

Clarissa nodded from the doorway. "I'll be waiting for your return. Just have a good time and don't worry about anything." *'I'll be doing enough of that for five people as it is,'* she added silently.

Clarissa walked down to the reception room with them and watched the three leave through the portal to the Faefardom Realm. As she continued to stare at the doorway, she felt iron bands wrap around her shoulders. She didn't think, just reacted. She elbowed her assailant, stomping on his foot. When the hold weakened with his grunt of surprised pain, she twisted and flipped him over her shoulder. It was only when he landed at her feet, staring wide-eyed up at her, that she realized who had placed his arm around her. She let his wrist go, taking a step back in abject horror.

"Mel! I'm so sorry. I hadn't realized!"

"I figured that one out myself. Thanks, darling. Love you, too." He stood and brushed off his suit. "Been a long while since you were that kinky."

She laughed as she swatted his belly. "Very funny. I was just mentally lost."

"I assume, then, the kids left on their field trip."

"Yes. Just minutes ago."

"They will be fine. Come on. I need you at the council. Coyote is going to be sentenced and I am sure you wish to be there for that bit of entertainment."

Clarissa nodded. "Yes. I hope he pays dearly for what he has done: taking our daughter, keeping her from us, tricking her by being this Nathan and deceiving her into trying to find the Gem of Avarice."

"I highly doubt the punishment would be as severe as we would like, but, something is better than nothing." Mel took her hand and they opened the portal to go to the council chambers where several of the gods were waiting for Nana and Coyote to return. Mel led Clarissa to the side area, pulling her chair out as she sat.

They had barely gotten situated when Coyote was led in, wearing a gilded armband which negated his powers. He glowered at Mel while sporting a relatively new black eye and split lip. Clarissa gave a questioning look to Mel who simply nodded, taking personal satisfaction on Coyote's injuries. Mel leaned over to her and added quietly, "He's lucky that was all I got a chance to give him. He's also lucky he didn't get two minutes alone with you. I think you would have done far worse." He rubbed his stomach where she elbowed him to make his point.

Nana entered the chambers before she got a chance to respond, but she continued to glare at Coyote in the meantime. Nana called the council back in session. He gave Clarissa a nod in acknowledgement of her presence before turning his full attention on Coyote.

"You have done many despicable things in your millennia of a lifetime, but never anything like this. Your search for the Gem of Avarice has exposed the treacheries committed, the least of which was arranging for the murders of Clarissa's family, conspiring with Jes to send Xon and others to obtain the stone and, finally, in the kidnapping of a child. You took the daughter of your friend, knowing they were worried for her safety. Your ambition to acquire the artifact has caused a callousness within you. The fact you didn't sexually touch her or physically harm her is your only saving grace."

Coyote grinned, almost as if in triumph, then frowned when he heard Nana's next words.

"However, that said, your crimes will not go unpunished. You have been spared the death penalty, but you will be incarcerated for one hundred years times how many years she was in your custody."

"Five hundred years? And just where do you plan on locking me up?"

"I'm so glad you asked. The Maurepas Realm has a wonderful detention camp. We know how much you love that realm and how you were able to get the Rougarou to work for you. However, you should be warned, it won't be the Rougarou who will be guarding you: it will be the Vacherie. To make sure you cannot influence the Rougarou or anyone else, you will be mostly kept in isolation in order to reflect upon your greedy transgressions."

Coyote visibly cringed. Clarissa had learned quite a bit during her years of searching the Maurepas Swamps to find her daughter, and she had come across the Vacherie in the process. She was pleased with the sentence. The Vacherie were even more fierce than the Rougarou. They were distant cousins to the winged Waia demons. The Vacherie were known for siphoning powers and using those powers as a form of punishment to the one they were siphoned from. Since Coyote was a god, his powers were virtually limitless. They all knew he would be tortured relentlessly with his own magic, whether in solitary confinement or not.

Once the sentence had been delivered, the other gods and goddesses began to move over to Mel and Clarissa, congratulating them on the safe return of Trinity, checking on her well-being and asking a myriad of other questions. Mel and Clarissa were polite enough to answer some of them before Mel extracted his wife and led her to Nana's chambers, knocking on his door.

"Come in, come in," they heard from inside. Mel opened the door for Clarissa, shutting it behind himself. Nana moved over to her and gave her a brief hug before shaking Mel's hand, then offering for them to sit.

"I called you in because we still have the issue of the shard of stone in Jasmine."

"I assumed we would be having a discussion about that," Clarissa said softly. This was not Mel's forte so he sat back, holding Rissa's hand to give her a silent strength. Before any could continue, a soft knocking came again.

"Enter Archanidou," Nana called out, just as she opened the door.

Spiderwoman greeted Clarissa and Mel before she moved to stand by Nana's chair.

"I feel like I'm in the principal's office," Clarissa said, looking back and forth between the two of them. She felt Mel squeeze her hand but it only reassured her slightly.

"We have been discussing Jasmine's predicament, as well as Trinity being used as she was," Nana started.

"Our children should not have to suffer for the greed of others. Your daughter will always be at risk, just as you were, Clarissa. Being hunted in order to be used to find any speck of the stone still in existence. My granddaughter will always be hunted for having a shard buried within her."

"What are you proposing?" Mel asked, totally unsure where this was leading. The fact that both his youngest child and his wife were being discussed had him a bit concerned.

Clarissa shifted uncomfortably in her chair, waiting for them to make their points.

Nana spoke. "We believe all of the pieces are safe from being found, with the exception of this one within Jasmine. Clarissa, you have been into almost all the realms but the human and Faefardom, and the only piece in the latter, we are already familiar with where it ended up. None were kept within the former since it could no longer be protected by you due to your circumstances." Nana didn't wish to bring up the fact she was killed specifically, knowing she would be well aware of what circumstances he was referring to. "Since you have not heard a calling anywhere else, we can safely assume the rest of the pieces, which were hidden by Archanidou's children, were successfully concealed."

"Agreed. However, I don't see the point you are trying to make other than pointing out the fairly obvious," Clarissa asserted, still skeptical.

"The point is, Clarissa, you can eliminate the last bit of stone without harming either of our families, but protecting them instead."

Mel and Clarissa looked at each other, surprise clearly on their faces. "What do you mean?" Mel asked the question, which was prominent with both of them.

Nana leaned forward, his elbows on his desk, his hands steepled in front of him, almost as if searching for the right words. When he finally spoke, he concentrated solely on Clarissa.

"As you are aware, your maternal lineage was given the responsibility for protecting the Gem of Avarice. You multi-great grandmother was chosen for her loyalty, her faithfulness, her fierceness and because she could not be swayed to use the power the gem offered. We knew her line of descendants would have the same attributes. We were also aware her special ability with the stone would also be passed down to each protector. Before you ask, no, it is not the ability to hear the stone when it calls, although it certainly helped, but that endowment didn't occur until the gem trusted its guardian and they developed a symbiotic relationship."

"So, then, what are you referring to? What power did she have, which has, supposedly, been passed genetically down to me?"

"You have the ability to absorb the power and quell it," Spiderwoman announced.

Clarissa's mouth dropped open and hung ajar for several moments. Mel appeared just as shocked. "Why didn't anyone know this?" he asked. "Why hadn't her line ever used it in order to stop being hunted and have some semblance of a normal life?"

"Mostly because they didn't know themselves," Nana responded. "As a leader of the pantheon, I've been privy to information unknown by others. Only the heads of the Elders Council were aware of her ability, which we discovered quite by accident."

"So why didn't you tell her and have her end such a threatening artifact?" Clarissa asked, still not fully believing what she was being told.

"It was not the gem's time, nor the time of the guardian," Nana replied cryptically.

"Explain," Mel growled softly, knowing to still be respectful to this man.

Although, it was Archanidou who answered. "It was prophesied eons ago of a precious gem which was begotten from the birth of the cosmos. It stated one protector would bear witness to the gem being dismantled when none would believe it possible. The power the artifact contained within would then be released into the atmosphere and rejoin with the cosmos."

Nana added, "However, there was a second possible outcome where the power sought would still exist. Therefore, the guardian needed to be chosen, not only from those candidates who would resist the call, but also be willing to sacrifice themselves to absorb it, should such a dire solution become necessary."

Mel stood up and leaned on Nana's desk, a deep furrow on his features. "Are you telling me, Rissa has to give up her life again to keep Trinity and Jasmine safe? If so, then our answer is fuck no! We will figure out something else."

Clarissa was on her feet almost as quickly, but instead of confronting Nana and Archanidou, she laid a gentle hand on Mel's arm. "No, Mel. No. If it keeps Trinity safe, and even Jasmine. If it keeps *our daughter* from ever being kidnapped or used by others like Coyote, then I will do it. For our daughter. For our family."

Before Mel could respond that he wouldn't have a family if not for her, and he was not about to lose her a second time, Nana spoke. "No. That's not what I am saying."

Both Mel and Clarissa turned to give him their full attention. Nana didn't speak until they both backed up and retook their seats. Once he knew they were calm enough to listen, he continued. "You are correct in your assumption. Clarissa would have perished if she or any of her ancestors had absorbed the gem's powers, for it would have been like taking a part of the creation of the cosmos within her body. She would not have been able to handle it. None of them could have, which is why we never let them know. Life is sacred and is never taken so lightly."

He could tell Mel was about to say something so held his hand up to keep him quiet. Once Mel settled down again he continued.

"The point being, this is not a whole gem we are talking about. It's only a sliver. An amount which should be able to be handled easily."

"You couldn't have started with that tidbit of info?" Mel grumbled.

"This is good news, babe." Clarissa reached over to him, taking his hand in hers. "I'll do it, but I am not sure how."

"I'll guide you," Archanidou stated confidently. "It sounds more difficult than it will be. We just have a few things to set up and then we will be ready for Jasmine."

"Does she know about this solution?" Clarissa asked.

"No. Not yet. I, myself, only learned of it just a short while ago," Spiderwoman responded.

"And I have been dealing with Coyote's culpability in this whole affair. I put it off until that venue had been completed," Nana added quietly.

"What if she says no?" Mel asked.

"Why would she?" Archanidou answered. "Regardless, she will see reason. It is for her protection and it will allow her the freedom she has always dreamed of. She won't say no."

Clarissa stood. "So when do we do this?"

"Tomorrow at noon. The sun must be at its apex for the day in the Human Realm."

Clarissa frowned. "Maybe you have forgotten, but I cannot go to the human world."

248

"True, but you can go to the Maurepas Realm. At noon, the barriers between the worlds will be down enough for you to siphon the cosmic energy you will need."

Clarissa nodded as Archanidou held out her hand. "Come with me to my home tonight. We have some practicing to do."

Clarissa stood and kissed Mel, leaving the men behind as she headed to Archanidou's residence to start the process of keeping Trinity and Jasmine safe.

While Clarissa was with Archanidou, Azamel headed back to his office. He needed a quiet moment to just think over everything which had occurred over the past months, the revelations exposed during the trial and more. He was glad he had warned Clarissa of Coyote's involvement with her family's deaths. It was already a tremendous shock coming from him, he couldn't imagine what would have happened had she been at the summoning to hear it first-hand. Mel rubbed his brow. The whole thing was fucked up.

When a soft knock came, he lifted his head and straightened his back to his normal regal pose. "Come."

Shara walked in, shutting the door behind her.

"How did things go?" she asked softly.

Mel shrugged. "Not as well as I would have hoped, but good enough. He is being locked in solitary for a few hundred years. Personally, I would rather have hung him by his fingernails for all he has suffered upon my family."

"Dying would have been too good for him, but sometimes, when one is used to having others around them, as well as coming and going as they please, having those things taken away is harsh indeed and more torturous than any physical pain."

"I suppose you are correct. Still, I would have loved to extract a pound of his flesh." He sat back and steepled his fingers in front of him. "However, I suspect that is not the full reason you are here."

It always unnerved her that Mel could read her so easily when no one else could. Probably because she has been with him so long, little idiosyncrasies even she didn't realize she had showed were like neon beacons to him.

"I was curious. After all, Trinity and Logan are almost like my own kids. I helped to raise them, have been with them almost every day of their lives. However, you are correct. I came for something else as well."

"Out with it."

"I wish to explore the possibility of…" She couldn't even say it. This had been her home for so long. To consider resigning her position and leaving was tumultuous at best.

"It's Mani. You want to leave and start a new life with him." Mel didn't ask, he stated. And, even though she shouldn't have been surprised, she was.

"Yes," she said softly.

"However, you also don't want to leave here. You feel safe."

Shara nodded. "Yes. But, I want to be with him."

"Is he around? Summon him here."

Shara paled then sent a mental link to have him visit Mel's office. Within moments, another knocked on the door. "Come," Mel commanded.

Mani stepped in, giving a quick glance to Shara before approaching Mel. He didn't say a word.

Mel gave Mani an appraisal before he spoke. "Where are you going to live?"

"Not sure. I was thinking we would look for a place in one of the other realms. Maybe the human one."

"How will you support her?"

Mani frowned. "I'll manage. I'll do what needs to be done to make sure she is taken care of. We just want to be together."

"Would you do anything?"

"If that is what it took. Yeah." Mani started to get suspicious.

"So, in reality, you two are just going to go bumbling about trying to make a living, fuck only knows where, or how, just so you two can be together?"

251

Shara noticed Mani looking over his shoulder at her. She looked nervous and fearful. If Mel said no, Shara wasn't sure she would be able to leave. Shara was aware Mani knew she had been with Mel for an extremely long time and Mel was making some good points. However, a life without Mani seemed worse. She began to wring her hands, something neither man had ever seen her do before.

"Request denied."

Mani's blood boiled and he slammed his hands down on the desk. "How dare you? How fucking dare you? Who the fuck are you to determine where and how she spends her life? She wants to be with me and I with her and that is the fucking end of that story."

Mani spun and grabbed Shara's hand to drag her away, but he couldn't get the door open and, when he tried to flash, he kept bouncing back. He spun on Mel. "What the fuck? Let us go."

"No. I was not finished."

Mani turned and crossed his arms, glaring at the demon judge.

"Shara has been with me a long time. I saved her and brought her here when her family was destroyed. I believe she feels safest here, and considering her reluctance to leave overall, I believe she is only going to remain with you. Therefore, I am offering an alternative. You can work for me as a guard and hunter. I have seen your work. You are persistent and over all good at what you do. In return, you and Shara may remain here under my roof. She will continue to be my assistant, you will be in my employ, you will both be safe with a roof over your head and the protection I can afford."

Mani's eyes narrowed. "Are you fucking with me?"

Mel chuckled. "Dude, you are not my type."

That statement caught them off guard and even Mani had to roll his eyes. "Thank the gods for small favors." Becoming serious again, he looked at Shara who gave one simple nod.

"We would be here together. Meals, necessities, whatever, we would work for?"

"You would have everything Shara enjoys now and more. I'll have a suite designed for the two of you and any additions you might have in the future. You will be in the realm where demons are welcome and you can be yourselves without harassment and, as stated already, you both would be protected."

"And if we say no? Then what? Or if we change our minds in the future?"

"Shara knows where the doors are. However, I felt it appropriate you at least hear the full offer before you stormed out. The choice is yours."

Shara didn't even give Mani a chance. "We'll take it. Thank you."

She then pulled Mani out of the office before either of the men changed their minds.

Mel smirked. If only all his decisions were as easy and had a happy ending.

## Chapter 22

When Clarissa arrived, Mel and Trinity accompanied her. They weren't necessarily needed, but the two insisted on coming for support, if nothing else. Clarissa admitted she was a bit nervous doing the absorption, yet she knew this was the right thing to do. Archanidou admitted to her during her training that the shard could contain more power than they were aware of, or her body might not be able to handle it all before she could quell it. There were a myriad of possibilities for something to go seriously wrong and Archanidou wanted to make sure Clarissa was aware of all the potential complications which could arise. At least, the ones they could contemplate. There were always unexpected dangers with something like this.

Clarissa was grateful Archanidou had not shared these hypotheses with Mel, for she knew him well enough to know he would have tried to forbid her to go through with it. Tried being the operative word. Succeed? Not so much. However, she didn't want Trinity to suffer any more than she had already and she could feel for Jasmine who carried this within her by a fluke, not by choice. She also was aware of how much Logan cared for this female and she would not have her son's heart broken if she could help it. She knew Jasmine would be hunted for the little sliver she carried by any who came near and could sense the bit of the stone. Like Clarissa, Logan had already suffered with the loss of his sister; she wouldn't risk doing that again to him with the woman he loved.

Arriving at the location on Maurepas, they saw Archanidou, Jasmine, Logan and Tyler awaiting them. Heading over to the three of them, they all exchanged greetings. Jaz, Logan and Trinity had spent a wonderful day touring the home of Tyler as he showed them many wonders. Trinity hated the idea of going, but found herself having a really wonderful time, mainly in part because of Tyler, who was overtly charming and attentive. Logan worried he was playing her, as he had so many other women, but gave him the benefit of a doubt and assumed he was just being helpful in order to get Trinity to enjoy herself and forget her captivity for even a few moments.

Trinity and Mel stayed out of the sacred circle, which had been drawn on the solid ground around a table. Logan was beside Jaz, keeping an arm securely around her. Tyler seemed to light up when he saw Trinity, but remained beside Archanidou in case he was needed. Clarissa turned to Mel and gave him a kiss before she moved inside the circle to stand by the table. Jasmine had some colored symbols drawn on her face, chest and arms. She knew they not only covered her torso fully, but the tendrils of lines also went down her legs. The lines represented the blood flow through her body, where the stone had influence.

"Let's get this over with," Jasmine said when all the pleasantries were exchanged. Looking back at her grandmother, she carefully entered the circle and got on the table, lying in a prone position. It made Logan nervous for she looked like she was about to be sacrificed to some Incan or Mayan god.

Trinity spoke up, watching as well. "Why is Jaz going through with this? I tried to do the same thing and almost killed her. How can you allow this to happen?"

Clarissa went over to her daughter and took her hands, her thumbs rubbing over the backs of them. "There is a difference, honey. Where you tried to extract the bit of stone so it would still be tangible and retain its power, I will be absorbing and nullifying it. Where you were trying to take it from her body, I am leaving it in, just taking its power. Does that make sense?"

"I think so." Trinity turned to Jaz. "I really am sorry I hurt you."

Jasmine shook her head. "You have nothing to be sorry about, for the hundredth time. I told you before, I don't blame you one bit. You didn't know what you were doing and you really didn't have a choice. However, I have a choice now and I would really like to get this over with. Please."

Clarissa nodded, letting Trinity's hands go. Moving within the circle, she stood over Jasmine's prone body. As she learned from Archanidou, Clarissa recited the words, closing her eyes, listening for the call of the stone and finding its center.

At first, no one was sure anything was going to happen. Then a soft orange haze began to arise from the lines and symbols drawn on Jasmine's body, coalescing towards Clarissa's mouth, being drawn in like a moth to a flame. Jasmine started to twitch and cry out so Logan began to rush into the circle but was held back by Archanidou.

"No. If you go in and try anything while it's only midway accomplished, you could irreparably damage them both. Let it play out. It will be okay."

Her words stopped Mel from crossing into the circle as well. He wasn't entirely sure this was the best thing for his wife to be doing, even though she told him it would be safe. He had to wonder what taking even a little bit of power into her body would do to her. How would it affect her? Would she change as a result? He began to pace, as if a caged animal, on the outside of the circle, waiting for the completion of the ceremony.

Although it seemed like hours, it was only minutes later when Clarissa collapsed and Jasmine remained still. Were either of them breathing? Archanidou pulled back her hand. "Go to her, child," she said. It was all the encouragement Logan needed as he dashed to the table and checked on Jasmine's vitals. Her pulse was weak, her breathing halted, but it was there. She was alive and he scooped her up into his arms, holding her close as his eyes followed his father and the identical actions for his mother.

Mel scooped Clarissa up from the ground, holding her still form against him. Images of the last time she was this still flashed through his mind. She had died in his arms and he would never in all his life forget that moment when he thought he had lost her for all eternity.

Even though there was a pulse, she was not responding to him. He became gut-wrenchingly fearful he was going to lose her again. He whispered soft words for her ear only, begging her to come back to him, not to leave him alone and how much he needed her, loved her. She was why he wanted to get up in the morning. She was the reason he found excitement in each day. She was the vindication he lived and didn't just exist. She was his everything.

Simultaneously, Jasmine and Clarissa gasped for air and awoke. Clarissa realized she was in Mel's arms and threw hers around his neck, clinging tightly to him. "Can we go home?"

Mel nodded to Trinity and said a thank you to Archanidou before transporting Trinity, Clarissa and himself back to his manor in the Nether Realm. He would talk to Logan later. Right now, his main concern was the woman he adored.

Logan continued to hold Jasmine until she pushed him away slightly. "Did it work?" she asked.

Logan was about to answer that he was sure it had from the light show which arose from her body, but then he realized her eyes were different. They were no longer filled with specks of a fiery orange and yellow. They remained a solid amber and he knew then, the stone's power was no longer an integral part of her.

"Yes, my child. It is gone. Clarissa succeeded in bringing it into herself and nullifying it. You are safe to go where you please and never have to worry about being hunted for your life's blood ever again."

"Thank you, Nunohum."

"How do you feel, Jazzy?" Tyler asked and they almost forgot he was there, standing as a silent vigil to all that occurred.

"I feel lighter, somehow. Freer. Like this heavy weight has been lifted from my body."

"In a way it has, Jasmine. You no longer carry within the power the gem contained. Even that minute amount must have been leaden inside of you. Head home. I will check on you in a while." Archanidou dematerialized, leaving the two men and Jasmine alone.

"Can we leave now? This place gives me the willies," Tyler grumbled. "And don't start that kissy lovey shit in front of me. I don't want to see that right now."

Logan cast him a *'shut it'* glance as he scooped Jasmine in his arms. She was about to complain, then realized it was nice to be carried, so she let him. Tyler didn't know he and Jasmine still hadn't gotten back to their former place in their relationship, so Ty didn't need to worry about being exposed to any lovey dovey stuff.

"Let's just go home," Logan said quietly. "Let's go home."

## Chapter 23

A week had passed since the ritual was performed and Jasmine was still getting used to her newfound freedom. No longer was she limited in the amount of time she could roam around the streets of New Orleans, or anywhere else she wanted to go. It was certainly liberating.

Tyler had taken Trinity out on Bourbon Street to see the sights. Although Trinity was concerned with the amount of people, she felt more secure with Tyler at her side. Before they left, Logan had pulled Ty away to speak to him privately.

"She's still so vulnerable right now, Ty. I don't want you messing around with her and dropping her like a used beer can when you are done, like you have with others. She couldn't handle it. She has been through too much as it is. Besides, she is my sister and I would take offense if you treated her with anything less than respect."

"I'm aware of that. I get where you're coming from, man, but I actually like her. She has been through a lot, but she has a strength of spirit that bastard never broke. I find such a quality admirable. I promise I am not going to use her in such a way. Ever." Tyler shifted uncomfortably, something Logan had never seen the cocky, self-assured male do before. "I really like her Logan. The only bad thing about her is she is related to you, but I can overlook that one flaw, if need be."

Logan was stunned. "Are you telling me you want to get serious with her?"

Tyler looked over at him. "Not at the moment. She is not ready for anything serious with anyone. Fuck, man. She just went through hell and more with Nathan and shit. She isn't going to trust anyone. I don't care, though. I want to be with her and help her through her tribulations. I want to stand by her side and maybe, somewhere down the road, if she feels like she can trust me and wants to be with me, yeah. I would like to get, as you say, serious with her. I will wait until she is ready though, no matter how long it takes."

Logan stared at him, taking him in with a securitizing look. He had to admit, living with Tyler for the past few years had gotten him to know the Fae pretty well and he had never seen him so serious before, except when they were about to go on the rescue for Trinity. He believed Tyler was telling the truth. Knowing how he protected Jazzy for most of her life, he had the utmost faith in Ty to protect his sister, even from himself if need be. Logan nodded and held out his hand. Ty took it and they shook, but Logan stepped up close. "You treat her well, 'cause if you don't, I will gut you like a pig for roasting. Got me?"

"Gotcha dude. No worries on that front. Promise. Besides, your father has already threatened to have me gelded should I attempt anything. I rather like my balls where they currently are and not on his wall for decoration."

"You talked to my dad?" Logan was surprised, though why, he wasn't quite sure. He should have known his father would be aware of everything to do with his daughter, as well as himself. He was also rather surprised his father was being so accommodating to Trinity and Tyler. He must have seen something in the latter which he admired and that was rare indeed. Mel also must have realized Trinity needed to have the freedom she had stolen from her all those years ago. Either way, he should not have been as astonished as he was.

"Yeah, dude. Shortly after the ritual. He called me to his office, like, hours later. Said he knew how I felt about his daughter and if I treated her right and didn't rush her, he would allow me a pass to visit her in the Nether Realm whenever I desired to. An open invitation. Can you fucking believe it? But then I also got the warning about my man parts and my wings being pinned on his wall as trophies should I hurt her in any way. Actually, the words were, 'make her angry or cause her to cry' and I was going to be missing my parts." He clutched his manhood protectively. "Dude, I like my junk and your old man is fucking scary."

Logan chuckled. "Yeah. He is to any who are not his family, and he has earned his reputation. I guess if he talked to you, then there is nothing else I can say which you would fear more."

Logan let him go so Tyler could get Trinity and show her around New Orleans. However, knowing he had the house for just him and Jasmine tonight got him thinking about a nice, quiet time together. She also had been through quite a bit and, ever since her amnesia, they had not fully returned to their previous state of commitment. Sure, Jazzy could remember their past and how much they cared about each other, but there was also the issue of her overcoming what she went through. She didn't care to be touched or kissed by Logan, much less anything else. Worse, she preferred he continue to sleep on the couch and not share the same bed. He hated not holding her when he fell asleep or having her cuddled against him when he awoke. He knew she also needed time and he was willing to give it to her, just like Tyler was doing for Trinity. He wouldn't push and would be there when she was ready to move forward again.

They shared a quiet dinner, enjoyed some romantic dancing with music from the radio and soon, Jasmine said she was ready for bed. He walked her to the room they once shared but, this time, she asked him to come in. He was a bit surprised but didn't hesitate, other than to ask if she was sure.

"Yes," was her only reply.

Logan was instantly nervous. He was unsure how far she wanted to go. Was it simply sleeping in the same room? Should he consider looking at the chair to sleep in or was she willing to share the bed? Should he hold her as she drifted off to sleep or establish a pillow barrier between them? He was still considering all the options on what to do when Jazzy moved to stand in front of him. She pushed him to sit on the bed, then began to slowly unbutton her blouse. Logan's eyes widened, hopeful and yet worried it might be too fast for her. Yet, she invited him in. She closed the door behind them and she was removing her garments. She had to know what this was doing to him. He didn't budge. He didn't breathe. He was scared this was all a dream or if he moved he would startle her enough she would disappear. So he remained still.

Logan watched as Jasmine took her outer clothes off, leaving a bra, panties and a garter attached to some silken stockings. His turquoise eyes darkened. Heat started radiating from every pore as he drank in the image of her. He couldn't stand the torture she was putting him through any longer. He stood and slowly stalked towards her, a low, heavy hum emanating from his chest as he growled out, "Mine."

He crashed into her, his hands exploring her soft skin, his lips pressing against hers, his tongue pushing past her lips to claim what was his. Logan's arms wrapped around her waist as he picked her up, turned and rushed towards the bed. Jasmine pulled his shirt off the first chance she got. She undid his belt while he kicked off his own shoes. She flipped him over, straddling him, and sat up. She moved her leg in such a way so that she could reach the garter straps, undoing them. Slowly, she rolled down the nylon stocking. It was her own hands touching her skin, but his lustful look made it almost feel as if it was his hands upon her leg. She could feel the moisture pooling between her legs, captured by the silky triangle of cloth which protected, if one could call it that, her sex. Moving again, she reversed her leg and repeated the process.

He was rock hard beneath her as he watched Jaz remove her stockings. He was doing his best to be patient, but she wasn't making it easy. Reaching behind her, she undid the bra, using her arms to block his view of her breasts as she removed it with one hand, dangling the garment to drop to the floor, along with everything else thus far. The only thing left were her panties, which were now a tad moist, and his jeans, showing an evident, tell-tale bulge. He continued to force himself to breathe evenly, despite his heart pounding in his chest. He was throbbing underneath her and Logan was going to soon become desperate. He reached up to work one breast, then the other, her moans causing him to react with more vigor in his attentions. Half lidded, her amber eyes were dark.

Jasmine undid his jeans as he lifted his hips up so she could slide them down. He kicked them off the rest of the way to end up in a pile on the floor with the rest of their clothing. He didn't bother to pull her panties down; he just tore them off, promising to buy her some new ones at a later date. At the moment, he only wanted to feel her soft skin against his.

She needed him to fulfill the ache deep within her core. She let him use her sex to rub against his, lubricating him and knowing soon her greatest need would be fulfilled. He flipped her over to be above her and, without any preamble, he drove himself inside her. Her slow striptease had kept him from taking her when he wanted, but as soon as she gave him the opening, Logan took it, making love to her hard and fast. It didn't take long with the pounding pace he had set upon before she was close and ready to succumb totally to him.

She clawed at him as her need increased to the point where she was blinded to everything but the completion of their union. He didn't slow down, thrusting into her relentlessly. He could feel her building underneath him and, when she finally gave herself over to him, they both came in a frenzied orgasm which left them both gasping for breath once it ran its course. It had been too long since they shared themselves as one, but this was the epitome of what he needed and desired most. Her. Being with her in every way imaginable. He knew, right then and there, she was his, but more importantly, he was hers. He would never want anyone else.

For the first time, he understood how his father felt about his mother. Jasmine was Logan's everything and he would protect her with his very life. Not that he wouldn't have previously, but something between them seemed to click like never before. Maybe because there wasn't the threat of his losing her over the gem inside of her. Maybe because she didn't have that albatross hanging over her head. Maybe because she felt more freedom than ever before and didn't feel as if she were a walking time bomb.

Regardless, something changed and he felt it. They both did, and now they could live out their lives in peace, solidifying their commitment to each other. He curled around her, kissing her gently, and asked the question he had a hundred times before.

"Will you be my wife?"

This time, however, her answer changed. "Yes."

Logan couldn't believe he heard right and asked her to repeat it. She smiled up at him. "I'm no longer a threat to myself or those I care for. So, my answer is yes."

"You have just made me the happiest man alive. I love you so much. Always and forever." He kissed her again and spent the night showing her just how happy she made him.

## Epilogue

Five years later:

Mel approached the door. He knew they were a bit late, but Clarissa hadn't quite been willing to leave the infirmary just yet. She waited as long as she could before Mel barked at her to get her ass in gear.

The door swung open before he had a chance to knock, so, tugging Clarissa, he entered the vast room of Nana's office. It was the only neutral place for this type of meeting. Nana was already seated behind his desk.

"You're late. I don't tolerate lateness," Nana grumbled.

"It's my fault. Santanya's water broke two hours ago and I just hated leaving her. I know it's her second child already, but you know I'm just so excited to have young ones running around the house again. My sincerest apologies for making everyone wait."

"The birth of a first child, or the two-hundredth one, is always an exciting time," Archanidou stated. "Your tardiness is forgiven."

Despite their lateness, Mel and Clarissa greeted the others quickly with hugs and handshakes before Mel took his official seat at the conference table. Jasmine and Logan moved over to his mother. Jasmine's own belly just starting to show a slight bump. Clarissa and Mel had just learned they were about to be grandparents and they could not be happier. When they found out that

Shara was also pregnant, Mel told Trinity to stay away from whatever those two were drinking. He was not ready to be a grandfather to his daughter's child, although he had to admit she was becoming radiantly beautiful as she matured, and Tyler has taken exceptional care of her, thereby keeping his balls and his wings.

Trinity was the reason they were at Nana's chambers. Tyler stood by her side, grasping her hand firmly in his. Over the past five years, Tyler has stood by her side, helping Trinity through the nightmares and horrors she had endured at the hands of Coyote and all his scheming. He guided her into a society she hadn't even been aware of and, though they lived very well together in the Human Realm, Tyler's duties were calling him back to Faefardom. The meeting was to abolish the treaty between the residents of the Nether and Fae Realms. At least, in-so-far as Trinity, her family and her close friends like Shara, Mani, Santanya and Zen.

King Metheun represented the Fae faction. Most of the details had already been worked out, it was just the formalization of the new treaty yet to be accomplished.

Clarissa had a chance to look over the final document as well. Since she was Mel's wife and listed as one of those allowed to visit Faefardom, she would be required to sign. As she looked it over, she frowned. "I can't sign this as is."

Mel, Nana and Metheun frowned. "May I ask why not?" Mel cautioned.

Clarissa pointed to a clause. "It states here, her parents, her brother, her friends listed and her soon-to-be niece or nephew, with an addendum to future nieces or nephews."

Mel nodded. "And the problem?" He was becoming slightly impatient. The men had worked very hard on this treaty to have it stopped at this late date. He also didn't relish not being able to visit Trinity in her new home.

"The problem is, it only lists her brother. Nothing about any future sisters or brothers she might have."

Mel snorted. "I don't think we need to worry about that now."

Clarissa placed her hand on her own stomach and shook her head no. "I'm afraid she does."

Everyone in the room just stared at her. Mel was aghast and speechless. Metheun barked out a laugh, startling them all. "Fair enough and easy to change." He pounded Mel hard on the back. "You sly dog."

Mel finally found his voice. "Why didn't you say something sooner?"

"I just found out," she replied. "Plus, you were so worried about Trinity drinking whatever Jaz, Tanya and Shara were, you didn't say anything about me, and I guess I found their magical elixir by mistake." She frowned, worried he would not be happy about her pregnancy. This was certainly not how she wanted to tell him.

Metheun laughed louder, as did the others in the room. Congratulations were bantered about as the two of them continued to stare at each other. Mel stood. "Make the changes. We will be right back."

He grabbed Clarissa's hand and pulled her back out of the room to where he could talk privately to her.

"Mel. I'm sorry. I wanted to tell you, but I wanted to do it right. It's been a long time since we were parents." She was nervous as he pulled her to an alcove and pushed her up against the wall.

"You're sure?"

Clarissa nodded. "It was confirmed yesterday."

"How far along are you?"

"Five weeks."

He didn't say anything, just stared at her and she was becoming sick to her stomach. Not in the morning sickness way, but the *'Oh my god, he hates me'* kind of way.

"I'm going to be a father again?"

"Um. Yeah. It *is* yours. Do you think I was with someone else?" she asked, confused.

"No. I am just trying to comprehend. I'm going to be a father again." He smiled as he leaned down, his lips inches from hers, his warm breath against her skin. "I couldn't be happier."

He pressed his lips softly against hers. His second kiss was more demanding, sensual and full of promised desire of what was to come: the untold pleasure yet to be fulfilled in order to show her how happy he really was.

He pulled back before things got too out of control. "We will finish this later and I will show you how excited I am when this is done."

"What about Tanya's baby?"

"I will wait to show you how excited I am you are growing another life that is a combination of you and me for as long as I need to, but not a moment more. Let's get back inside and finish this up."

Smiling, they reentered the conference room and finished signing the treaty before returning back to their home to start planning for the arrival of so many bundles of joy.

## APPENDIX

Pantheon:

| Name: | Nickname: | Realm: |
|---|---|---|
| Nanaboojoo | Nana | High God: Protector of Humanity: Forests |
| Geezhigo-Quae | Gee | Sky Mother |
| Chipiapoos | Chip | God of the Dead |
| Beloitah | | Goddess of Evil |
| Malsumis | Mal | God of Evil |
| Azamel | Mel | Demon Bashing/Demon Judge/Executioner |
| Coyote | | Trickster |
| Archanidou | Spiderwoman | Goddess of Dreams/Dream Catchers |
| Michabochel | Micha | God of Water |
| Dahdahwat | Dah | God of Animals |
| Ictinike | | God of War |
| Deganiwada | Degan | God of Peace |
| Hino | | God of the Sun |
| Apisirahts | Apis | Moon Goddess |

| | | |
|---|---|---|
| Hamedicus | Ham | God of Time |
| Nokomis | | Goddess of Crops/Mother Earth |
| Crow | | God of Childbirth |
| Ockebewis | Ocke | Messenger God |
| Manitumis | | God of Sleep |
| Jes'Sakkid | Jes | God of Malignant Man |
| Genetaska | Gene | God of Justice |
| Janis | Jan | Goddess of Justice |
| Wabasso | Bass | God of Fire/Wolf Lord of Spirit Realm |
| Chakekenapok | Chake | God of Winter/Ice |
| Gaoh | | God of the Winds |
| Heng | | God of Thunder |
| Gawaunduk | Gawa | God of Love |
| Halinois | Hali | Goddess of Love |
| Hastseoltoi | Hasti | Goddess of the Hunt |
| Dzhihibai'Manido | Mani | Demon Spirit |

## ABOUT THE AUTHOR

Ms. Hawks has always been interested in writing in some form or other. A few years back, she was involved with and then ran a Star Trek Interactive Writing Group which was successful for a number of years. Yes, she is a trekker and proud of it.

She has directed tours around the country and continues to do so to pay the bills. Maybe one day, she can travel for fun and let the books she writes pay the bills instead. She can only hope.

A few years back, she received her Master's Degree in Ancient Civilizations, Native American History and United States History.

It was at this time she got involved in role playing on Facebook, which gave her ample opportunities to grow and hone her writing ability.

## More From Laura Hawks

http://www.amazon.com/Demons-Kiss-Demon-Saga-
Trilogy-
ebook/dp/B00S8SPQ78/ref=tmm_kin_swatch_0?_encod
ing=UTF8&qid=1462076150&sr=1-1

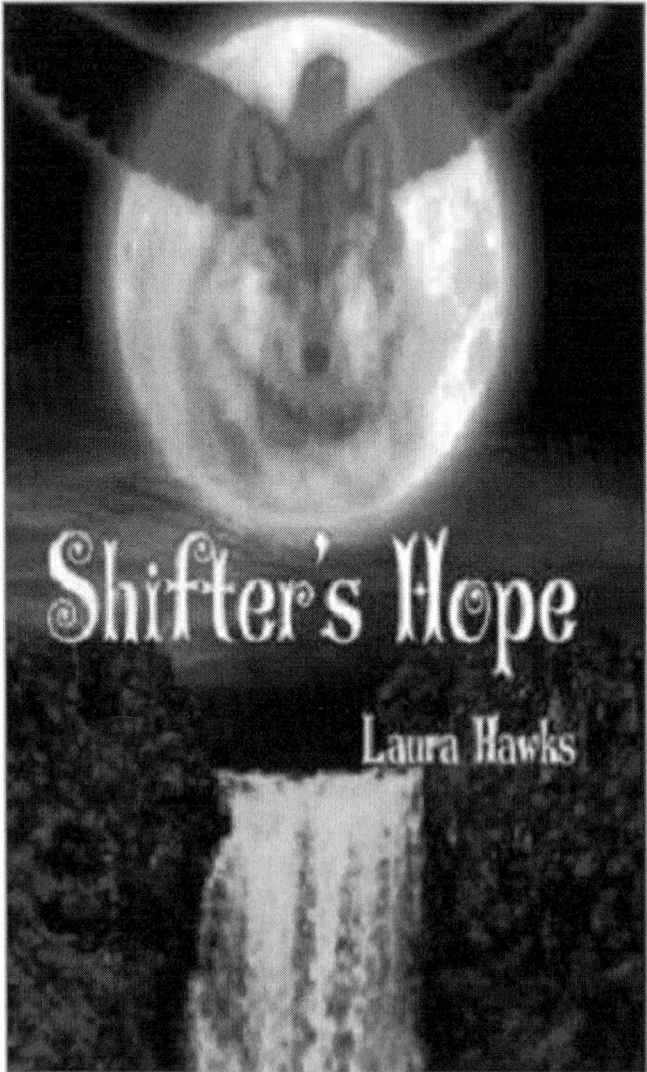

# The Ghost and the Grimoire

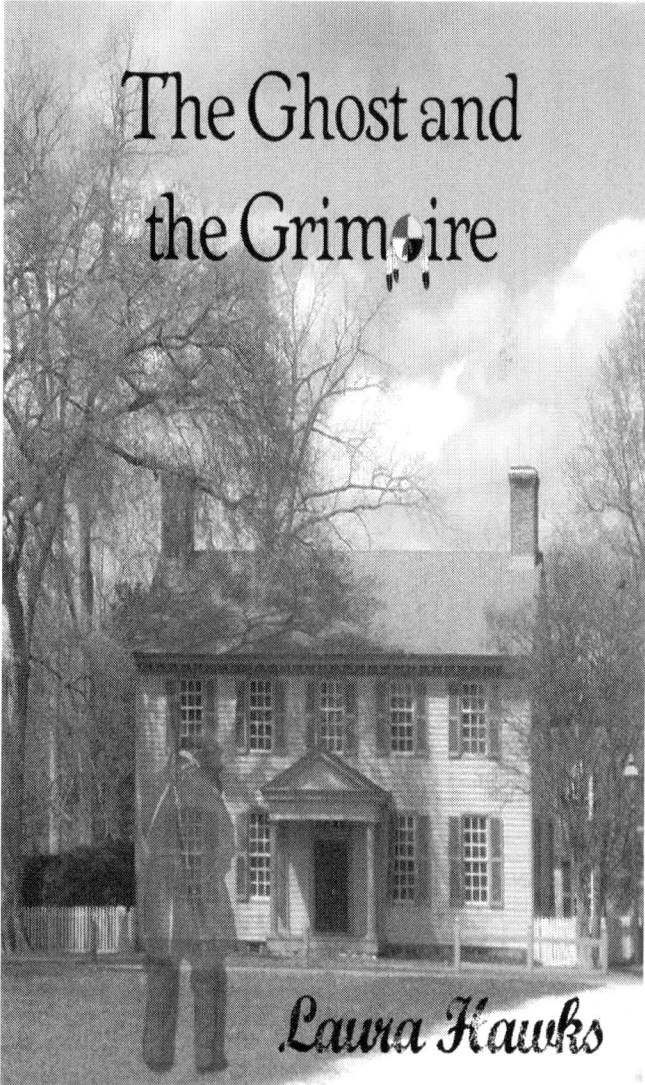

*Laura Hawks*

Printed in Great Britain
by Amazon